Sandblast!

I want my mummy . . . NOT!

'Shhh!' James held up his hand for silence. For a moment all they could hear was the sound of their own breathing.

Then, from beyond the sealed door, there came the scraping noises. James felt the hair on the back of his neck begin to rise. No one had entered the other room in over three thousand years. All that should be inside was the pharaoh's mummy – and that should definitely not be moving around!

JOHN VINCENT

Sandblast!

FANTAIL

FANTAIL BOOKS

Published by the Penguin Group
Penguin Books Ltd, 27 Wrights Lane, London W8 5TZ, England
Penguin Books USA Inc., 375 Hudson Street, New York, New York 10014, USA
Penguin Books Australia Ltd, Ringwood, Victoria, Australia
Penguin Books Canada Ltd, 10 Alcorn Avenue, Toronto, Ontario, Canada M4V 3B2
Penguin Books (NZ) Ltd, 182–190 Wairau Road, Auckland 10, New Zealand

Penguin Books Ltd, Registered Offices: Harmondsworth, Middlesex, England

First published in the United States of America by Puffin Books 1992
Published by Fantail 1993
1 3 5 7 9 10 8 6 4 2

Fantail Film and TV Tie-in edition first published 1993

Typeset by Datix International Limited, Bungay, Suffolk
Filmset in 12/13½ pt Monophoto Times
Printed in England by Clays Ltd, St Ives plc

CHAPTER 1

River Rats

The ancient steamboat chugged away from the dock and into the Nile River. James Bond Jr leaned against the railing of the boat and watched the town of New Kalabsha fade into the distance. He knew that as their boat steamed southward they would be leaving behind most traces of the twentieth century. By the time they reached their destination, they would have stepped back in time over three thousand years.

It was hard to imagine a place more different from England than this. Just two days before, James and his friends had been studying at Warfield Academy. Now, here they were – in the sticky heat of Egypt, on their way to an archaeological dig.

James could see his reflection in the clear water of the Nile: wind-ruffled brown hair, blue eyes, a half-smile on his mouth, all topped with a bright white pith helmet to keep the hot sun from giving him heatstroke. The khaki short-sleeved shirt and shorts and the hiking boots he wore were comfortable, no matter how weird they looked.

'What's wrong, Bond?' asked a sneering voice. 'Seasick already?'

James sighed and looked around. Trevor Noseworthy was standing behind James with his nose in the air – as usual. Trevor was a member of a respected English family and he was always talking about how important his father was. To make matters worse, he did this bragging in a voice that reminded James of fingernails scratching a blackboard. He was constantly trying to get James into trouble with Mr Milbanks, the headmaster of Warfield Academy. Most of the time Trevor's schemes backfired, and he was the one who wound up in detention – not James.

'Come on, Trevor,' James said. 'Can't you lay off and try to be friendly, at least while we're in Egypt?'

'I'd sooner be friends with one of those crocodiles,' Trevor spat, waving at the reptiles basking by the riverbank. He stalked off, leaving James alone at the ship's railing. Trevor would never change.

'Enjoying the view, James?' An elderly man approached him. His skin was tanned and wrinkled from the fierce Egyptian sun. He had a bushy white moustache but almost no hair on his head. His suit was neat and black, and instead of a pith helmet like the one James wore, he had on a traditional red fez.

'Yes, Professor Gheeza,' James replied. 'It really is spectacular.'

The Professor joined him at the railing. 'It is indeed,' he agreed. 'I've made this trip many times, but I never tire of gazing at the Nile.' He pointed to the grain fields they were passing. 'The river provides us with soil and water to grow crops. It has been this way with my people for thousands of years. Things change slowly in Egypt.'

James smiled. 'I guess some things are worth preserving. By the way, I really would like to thank you for letting us help you on this new dig of yours.'

Professor Gheeza shook his head. 'No, it is I who must thank you and your friends. There are few volunteers willing to help out scientists like myself.'

James was about to reply when he noticed that two men in dirty white suits had come onto the deck from the forward cabin. They were making their way towards James and the Professor. Both men had drooping black moustaches, shaggy hair, and straggly beards. And both were reaching into their jacket pockets.

Since starting school at Warfield Academy, James had run into more than his fair share of trouble. It wasn't that he asked for it – most of it had simply landed in his lap. Trusting his instincts, James just knew these characters were trouble.

'Do you know these men, sir?' he asked the Professor.

Professor Gheeza turned to look at the men. He, too, seemed to realize that they were up to no good. 'No, I don't know them,' he said, shaking his head. 'And I don't think I want to know them.'

Now that they had been spotted, the pair of strangers came to a sudden halt. Nodding at each other, they pulled their hands from their pockets and rushed at the Professor. Both of them had long, curved knives ready to stab the old man.

'Betrayer of your people!' the first man screamed. 'Die!'

James grabbed a lifebelt from the railing. With a flick of his wrist, he sent it spinning towards the closer thug. As the man threw up his hand to shield his face, his knife sank into the ring. The rope from the lifebelt tangled in his feet, and he fell to the deck with a muffled cry.

The second man leapt in the air, screaming wildly. He waved his knife around, trying to force James backwards. James pulled off his pith helmet and jumped between the assassin and the Professor. As the killer struck out with his knife James thrust his hat in the way. With a dull thud, the knife pierced the helmet.

'My hat's off to you,' James remarked as he jerked it to one side, yanking the knife from the killer's grip. Then he noticed the first man was back on his feet. Fighting the two men at once might be a real problem.

In one motion, James dived through the legs of his second attacker and grabbed the rope

4

from the lifebelt that was tangled around the feet of the other thug. He pulled on the rope as hard as he could.

With a wild cry, the thug crashed backwards through the boat's railing. There was a huge splash as the man hit the water. Holding on to the lifebelt, James got to his feet and turned to the other assassin.

The second killer ignored James and seized Professor Gheeza by the throat. He was trying to strangle the old man. James sneaked up behind the thug and slipped the lifebelt over his head. Then James pulled the ring down as hard as he could. The killer found his hands torn away from his victim and pinned tightly to his sides.

'Now I know why they call them lifebelts!' James said with a laugh. Then he used the rope to spin the attacker around. James gave the man a good kick in the seat of his pants and watched as the thug staggered across the deck and pitched headfirst over the side. 'At least he won't drown with that thing on,' James said. Then he turned back to Professor Gheeza.

The old man was gasping but on his feet. 'Thank you, James,' he wheezed. 'I don't know what I'd have done if they had caught me alone.'

'I'm glad I could help,' James told him. 'But I wonder what they were after.'

The Professor shrugged. 'Probably just

river bandits,' he said. 'There are sometimes problems with them robbing the tourists, I'm afraid.'

'If that were the case, they'd have attacked me,' James pointed out. 'I'm obviously the tourist here. But they were clearly after you.' He bent to pick up his helmet and pulled the knife from it.

The blade was curved and well polished. The handle of the knife was ivory and had small symbols carved into it. James recognized the figures as hieroglyphs – ancient Egyptian writing.

'Does this mean anything to you?' he asked, showing the knife to the Professor.

The Professor's eyes widened as he examined the blade. 'These are the ancient markings for *Pharaoh*,' he said, 'similar to those on other items that have been found in the pyramids. I'm sure you know that *pharaoh* is what the kings of old were called. There have been no pharaohs in Egypt for two thousand years. Yet . . . this blade is new. See? Stainless steel. This knife could not have anything to do with a real pharaoh.'

'That is so, Professor,' said a girl's voice. 'But there have been those who rob the sacred tombs of the pharaohs of old – like that young man you're talking to!'

CHAPTER 2

Veiled Threats

James turned around quickly. A young girl stood on the deck. She was wearing a traditional *chador*, or floor-length dress, of bright red cloth. The fabric veiled her face and hair as well. James could see only the bridge of her nose and her eyes, which were a deep blue, like the waters of the Nile.

Professor Gheeza smiled at her fondly. 'James, may I introduce my best student, Miss Cleo Daway.'

James gave Cleo a smile of his own, but it didn't seem to melt the ice in her eyes. 'My name's James – James Bond Jr.'

'As far as I'm concerned,' Cleo replied, 'all foreigners have only one name: *thief!* Like all of the rest, you are here only to loot the treasures of my country's past.'

'You're judging me rather fast – and unfairly,' James objected. 'I assure you, my friends and I are here solely to help Professor Gheeza.'

'Cleo,' Professor Gheeza said gently, 'believe me, James and his friends are here to help. They know that anything we discover in the tomb belongs to Egypt.'

The young girl seemed a little less tense, but there was still no welcome for James in her eyes. 'Englishmen have taken so many priceless objects back to their museums over the years,' she said. 'It is hard to believe any good even of one of them.'

'Then I hope to change your mind,' James told her.

'Perhaps I have spoken hastily,' Cleo replied. 'But we shall have time to get to know each other better. Maybe then my opinion of you will change.'

'I hope so,' James said. 'I'm all for international cooperation.'

The door to the forward cabin opened again. For a second James tensed, ready for action. He relaxed when he saw it was only Gordo and IQ.

IQ – the nickname everyone gave to Horace Boothroyd – was the resident genius of Warfield Academy. His active mind was always dreaming up new gadgets or plans, some of which worked and some of which caused spectacular disasters. He looked like an absent-minded professor with his thick glasses and messy blond hair. He had on his bright red Warfield school tie, along with the standard khaki clothing and pith helmet.

Gordon 'Gordo' Leiter was huge and muscular. He had long blond hair and a deep surfer's tan. He was dressed the same as James but instead of hiking boots he wore fluorescent hightops. As soon as he caught sight of Cleo his eyes opened wide.

8

'Whoa! Who's the mummy?' he said cheerfully. Ignoring the chilly look she gave him, he added, 'Did you have an accident, or don't you want to catch any rays?'

'Gordo,' Professor Gheeza said patiently, 'Miss Daway is dressed in traditional costume.'

'Hey, I'm from the U.S. of A., Prof,' Gordo replied. 'And bikinis and jams are traditional for this kind of weather.'

'Well, you are not in America now,' Cleo said coldly. 'Good day.' She strode off, leaving Gordo looking puzzled.

'What's with her?' he asked. 'I only asked a question.'

Professor Gheeza shook his head. 'Miss Daway believes very strongly in the traditions of our country,' he explained. 'She feels, perhaps rightly, that we may learn a lot from our own past.'

'Me, I'll stick with the present,' Gordo said.

James had to smile. 'I know what you mean, Gordo,' he agreed. 'But we probably *can* learn a lot from the past. To ignore it could be dangerous. And, speaking of dangerous, two thugs just tried to attack the Professor.'

'Yes,' added Professor Gheeza. 'If not for James, I might now be dead, my body floating in the Nile.'

James handed IQ the knife he'd taken from his hat. 'Maybe you could take a look at this,' he suggested. 'It belonged to one of the two

9

men. Maybe it will tell us something about them.'

Gordo peered at the sharp blade. 'Ouch! It already tells me something. We may be in for mega trouble on this trip!'

'You could be right, Gordo,' James replied. 'So keep your eyes open for anything out of the ordinary.'

Gordo nodded. Then, his brows raised, he pointed to a spot in the river ahead of the boat. 'You mean like a periscope?'

The others turned to look. Gordo was right. The thin black rod of a periscope rose out of the water about a hundred yards upstream from their ship.

'Yes,' James said drily. 'That's the kind of thing I mean.'

'James!' IQ cried. 'Look!'

As they watched, the periscope seemed to shudder. In the water ahead of it, a V-shaped wake appeared. Something was speeding through the river and heading directly for their boat.

'Heads up!' Gordo yelled.

'They've fired a torpedo at us!' IQ exclaimed.

CHAPTER 3

Bond Overboard!

James glanced over the side of the boat and turned to Gordo. 'Get up to the wheelhouse,' he ordered. 'Make sure the captain sees the torpedo and takes evasive action!'

'On my way!' Gordo agreed, already hustling.

'Can he possibly get there in time?' asked Professor Gheeza. 'There are a lot of people on this boat. And the boat itself turns so slowly!'

'Just in case he doesn't,' James said, 'I'm going to hitch a faster ride!' He hopped up on to the railings and leapt out over the river. Just as he was about to hit the water, his hands caught hold of the side of a passing speed-boat.

At the wheel of the boat, a middle-aged man with a large stomach stared at James open-mouthed.

'Sorry about coming aboard like this,' James said, plopping down into the seat beside the driver, 'but I need a lift.' He pointed ahead of them. The skipper's jaw dropped even lower.

'Torpedo!' he cried.

'I know,' James said patiently. 'We've got to intercept it before it hits that boat or dozens of people will be killed!'

The skipper just shook his head wordlessly. He opened his mouth to say something, but nothing came out. He looked frantically from side to side. Finally, in a total panic, he jumped overboard!

James watched the man swimming quickly for shore and clicked his tongue.

'Okay, okay,' he said. 'Since you insist, I'll steer.'

The torpedo had been moving steadily and was now dangerously close to the crowded ferry. James knew the only way to throw the deadly missile off track was to make it hit something else first. But what?

James sighed. 'Oh, well,' he said, 'easy come, easy go.' He steered the speedboat directly into the path of the oncoming torpedo. He threw one leg over the side before pushing both throttles all the way forward. Then, just as the boat began to shoot ahead, James dived off and began swimming furiously towards the ferryboat.

A moment later there was a tremendous roar and a blinding flash of light as the torpedo exploded on impact with the speedboat. James felt an overpowering pressure in the water around him and found himself hurled headlong into the air by a tremendous wave. His head was spinning, his ears were ringing,

and his body ached from the force of the blow.

Then he was slammed back down into the frothing waters. His breath was knocked out of him and he began to sink to the bottom of the Nile. He tried moving his arms and legs, but nothing happened. His head was spinning, and his body was paralysed. If he didn't start moving in a few seconds, he would drown!

As he hit the bottom of the river he felt a pair of arms wrap around him. Someone was pulling him upwards. Within seconds his head broke the surface. James gulped air into his lungs and felt his strength slowly returning. He looked behind him to see who had rescued him.

It was Tracy Milbanks. Her neat light-weight suit was soaked and her dark hair looked like stringy rats' tails plastered to her face. But she was grinning at him in relief.

'Thanks, Tracy!' he gasped. They began to swim back to the ferry.

'IQ told us what you were doing,' she called back. 'I saw you go under, and it looked like you needed a hand.'

'And I'm very glad you gave me two,' James said.

Several thankful passengers helped pull them aboard and handed them towels. IQ and Professor Gheeza rushed over to them. IQ had his portable computer and something that looked like a large microphone.

'James! You're all right!' he cried. 'Something amazing has happened,' he went on, holding up the gadget. 'This is my portable sonar. I brought it to help locate rooms in the tomb when we dig. Well, I just used it to try and track the submarine that fired on us.'

'And?'

'It's vanished. According to my readings, there's nothing in the water – anywhere!'

James frowned. 'It couldn't have passed us, and it could hardly have gone up the river this quickly. I wonder what –' He broke off as two more people pushed through the excited crowd that had gathered around them.

Trevor Noseworthy smiled nastily when he saw James. 'I always knew you were a big drip, Bond,' he sneered.

'Quiet, Noseworthy,' Mr Milbanks snapped. He'd been below during all the commotion, but by now he had heard – and seen – enough. 'I suppose you have an explanation for that explosion I heard, not to mention why you and my daughter were in the water?'

If Mr Milbanks knew that someone had tried to kill Professor Gheeza, he would certainly cancel the dig and insist that they fly back to England immediately. Apart from the fun they might miss, James suspected that the Professor might still need their help. 'Well, sir,' he began, 'it was just one of those lunatics in a speedboat. He came a bit close and knocked Tracy and me overboard. These kind people pulled us back.'

'I see. And the explosion?'

'I think he ran into something, sir. Luckily, he abandoned ship first.'

Mr Milbanks looked at him suspiciously for a moment. Then he sighed. 'I expect that's as much as I'll get out of either of you. It just seems odd to me that you're always around whenever there's some sort of trouble.'

James shrugged. 'I guess it's just bad luck.'

Shaking his head, Mr Milbanks went back to the cabin. IQ turned to James, a worried look on his face.

'What do you think all of this means?' he asked.

James stared thoughtfully at the hills the boat was chugging past. 'I think Egypt's got a big secret for us to uncover,' he answered. 'And I think there might be a lot more trouble coming our way on this little expedition.'

CHAPTER 4

Dig It!

Their boat docked in Luxor without any more problems. James, I Q, Tracy, Gordo, and Phoebe Farragut – the final member of the group of friends – hauled their luggage onto the wooden dock. Phoebe had twice as many bags as any of her friends. Her father was a wealthy businessman, and he didn't seem to mind her constantly spending his money. Trevor stood by himself about ten feet away from the group, trying to pretend he didn't know them.

Mr Milbanks, Professor Gheeza, and Cleo were among the last to leave the boat. As they walked over to the group an old, battered truck wheezed and sputtered its way to the dock. The driver hit the horn several times as he pulled to a stop.

'That's my assistant, Farid,' Professor Gheeza said, waving to the man. 'He has brought the truck to take us to our hotel. After you have settled in, we will visit the tomb and begin work.'

Cleo turned her stony gaze on James. 'And while we are there I shall take great care that you and your friends do not walk away with anything you should not.' Turning her back on them, she strode to the truck.

'Charming,' Phoebe said. 'I hope we don't see much more of *her*!'

James couldn't resist a smile. 'Speak for yourself, Phoebe. I wouldn't mind getting to know Miss Cleo Daway better.'

Later that afternoon Farid, a big grin on his sunburned face, was driving like a madman through the narrow streets of Luxor. Cleo rode with him in the truck's cab. James and his companions sat in the back, listening to Professor Gheeza as he pointed out the sights and explained things to them.

'This town is called Luxor nowadays,' he told them. 'But in classical times it was known as Thebes. It was the capital of Egypt for hundreds of years, most notably during the Eighteenth Dynasty.' He gave them a smile. 'I'm sure you've heard of King Tutankhamun and the wonderful artefacts found in his tomb. Well, he was just a minor pharaoh in his day, so you can imagine some of the treasures a really great pharaoh might have been buried with. Finding an intact tomb would be like opening an incredible, priceless treasure chest. But there are very few chances of ever doing that.

'Most of the tombs have been broken into by grave robbers – some just a few years after they were sealed. The lure of gold has tempted many people over the centuries, so we must not expect too much from the poor little tomb I have found.'

'I'd hardly call it that, Professor,' IQ objected, excitement in his eyes. 'It's the legendary lost tomb of Amenhotep I, the second king of the Eighteenth Dynasty and the first man to build a tomb cut out of rock instead of a pyramid. Even if it's completely bare, you've earned a place in the history books.'

'Thank you,' the Professor said. 'It would be nice to think this.'

After they crossed the river by ferry they all fell silent, staring in astonishment at the sight of one of the ruins on the other side. Two huge, broken statues poked out of the edge of the river, almost a hundred feet tall. 'The Colossi of Memnon,' Professor Gheeza told them. 'According to legend, they are supposed to scream at sunrise.'

'I'm not surprised,' Gordo muttered. 'I don't like getting up in the morning, either.'

Once they drove past the statues and the remains of several ancient temples, the road turned to the left and led into the hills. They couldn't help gasping at what lay before them. Cut directly into the rock of the hills was a massive temple with several rows of pillars and ramps leading up to it. Immense statues littered the hillside, and the ruins were surrounded by huge stone cliffs.

'Awesome!' Gordo breathed.

'The temple of Queen Hatshepsut,' the Professor told them. 'In ancient Egypt, the pharaohs were supposed to be men. When Hatshepsut came to power, she wore a ceremonial false beard to make her more acceptable to the people.'

'Weird,' Phoebe said. 'I'm glad that we live in a time when men and women are equals.'

'Yes,' IQ said. 'You wouldn't look too good with a beard!'

The truck continued to climb the steep hills.

'We're heading for the Valley of the Kings,' Professor Gheeza explained. 'There are two forks – the East Valley and the West Valley. We're going into the East, where most of the famous tombs are. That's where King Tut was buried.'

The truck bounced along the rocky road. Although the engine sounded like it was ready to give out any minute, they finally made it to the valley. Signs pointed the way to some of the tombs, but the Professor and Farid led them to a quieter spot off-limits to tourists.

Here there was a large pit dug into the ground. Around it were a number of tents for the workmen and their supplies. They approached the pit and gazed down into it. Part of a wall and a doorway had been uncovered. A camera and a tripod had been set up to record the opening of the tomb. Several of the local workmen were standing around, muttering under their breath.

'Man!' Gordo sighed, taking off his pith helmet and mopping his forehead. 'This heat really stinks!'

Professor Gheeza smiled. 'Actually, when excavating a pharaoh's tomb, the correct word is *sphinx*.'

'So flunk me,' Gordo muttered.

The Professor led the small party down into the excavation area. James noticed several tables set up with preservatives, bottles, labels, brushes, and any other equipment they could possibly need in case they discovered anything inside the tomb.

Farid used the camera to get several shots of the hieroglyphs carved into the stone doorway and the tomb's seal. The Professor explained that it was better to photograph inscriptions in the afternoon, to take advantage of the shadows cast by the late-day sun. 'The carvings become more readable,' he told them.

'Not to me,' James admitted. 'What does it say here?'

The Professor shrugged. 'Oh, it's just a curse promising horrible, violent deaths to anyone who opens this tomb. The usual sort of thing.'

'I don't understand,' James said. 'What kind of curse is it?'

'The curse of the pharaoh,' Professor Gheeza told him. 'When these tombs were sealed, the seals were routinely protected by the placing of terrifying curses. Think of it as one of those burglar alarm stickers people use. It's meant to give thieves a second thought. Really, it means nothing. Hundreds of tombs with this sort of seal have been entered, and no proof of a real curse has ever been found.'

The workmen muttered grimly all the while Gheeza spoke.

Suddenly the assembled workmen started to shout. James couldn't understand a word they were saying, but he saw the Professor's face turn red with anger.

'Come now,' the Professor called out. 'Surely you men do not believe such superstitious nonsense.'

The men obviously did, because they backed away from the door and continued to shout. Farid, looking a little embarrassed, turned to the Professor.

'They believe this curse *is* real,' he explained.

'They have heard strange rumblings underground. Some have seen what they say is the pharaoh's mummy walking the hills at night.' He spread his hands. 'I myself do not believe it – but they do.'

'Sounds like they've been watching too many late-late shows on TV,' Tracy said. 'That sort of thing comes from Hollywood, not Egypt.'

'Right,' IQ agreed, joining the Professor at the stone doorway. 'Fortunately, we men of science don't believe in nonsense like that!'

'Quite right,' Professor Gheeza said. He walked over to the table and picked up a hammer and chisel. Ignoring the gasps of fear from the workmen, he held the chisel over the seal. Then he gave it a firm crack with the hammer. The seal disintegrated.

IQ turned to face everyone, a big smile on his face. 'You see?' he told them. 'There's absolutely nothing to worry about.'

A sudden grating noise behind him made him jump. The door was opening – and there was nobody touching it! For a second no one moved.

Then a pair of hands shot out of the dark tomb. One grabbed IQ and the other fastened onto Professor Gheeza. With startled cries, both were yanked off the ground and pulled inside. The dark space of the doorway was eerily silent.

CHAPTER 5

Tomb It May Concern

It was true James had been expecting trouble, but not from inside a sealed, three-thousand-year-old tomb. He turned around and dashed through the stone doorway into the inky blackness within. Tracy and Phoebe followed. Farid hesitated, and the workmen ran away, terrified.

Inside, it was pitch black. James called out for IQ, but he couldn't see anything in the darkness. He knew they couldn't risk going any further until they could see what lay ahead of them. He didn't want any of them to accidentally break some priceless relic. Or worse, trigger some kind of nasty booby trap.

'Someone get a light,' he called over his shoulder.

There was the sound of a match being struck, but not from behind. It was from farther in the tomb. Suddenly, the whole room became visible.

They were standing in a passageway that led down into the ground. The hieroglyphs covering the walls and ceiling had been painted in bright colours that seemed not to have faded a bit since they had been placed there three thousand years before. Scattered on the floor were gold statues, wooden carvings, ancient weapons, and ornate, gilded chairs. It was obviously a very rich tomb! But James didn't pay any attention to the treasures for more than a second or two.

In the centre of the tunnel he could see IQ and Professor Gheeza. They were being held, squirming, off the ground by a huge man. Beside him was a second man, smaller and skinnier. Both were dressed in military uniforms with daggers in their belts and red caps on their heads. The second man held a small bundle of dynamite in one hand – with a lit fuse!

'Tomb robbers!' Tracy gasped.

The small man smiled crookedly. 'You should have paid attention to that ancient curse,' he told them. Then, with a nasty laugh, he threw the flaming bundle of explosives right at them.

James and the two girls ducked. The dynamite flew over their heads.

At that moment, Trevor strode into the tomb. By reflex, he caught the explosives in one hand. Without looking at what he had caught, he said, 'I don't carry torches for anyone.' He cocked his arm to throw it back.

'Trevor!' James yelled urgently. 'It's dynamite! Get rid of it!'

Trevor looked down at the bundle in horror. 'Dynamite?' he squeaked. Then his eyes rolled

up into his head and he fainted. The explosives continued to fizzle on the ground beside him.

'Some help he is,' Phoebe muttered.

While everyone stared at the hissing, sparking explosives, the two robbers moved. The tall one threw IQ and the Professor against the wall, dazing them. Then both men bolted for the open door. They shoved James, Phoebe, and Tracy aside and leapt over the dynamite.

Gordo and Cleo were just outside the tomb. The two men came flying out, bowling both of them over as they ran for their lives.

Inside the tomb, James dived for the dynamite. There were only a couple of inches of fuse left to burn. Then the bundle would explode. 'We've got to get this out of here,' he said, looking around the room desperately. His eyes fell on one of the ancient weapons he had seen earlier, a bow and arrow, and he reached for it. Maybe he could use it to launch the dynamite safely out of the tomb. But over the years the bowstring had rotted to nothing.

'Hurry, James!' Phoebe cried. 'I'm not ready for the afterlife!'

James couldn't see any way to get rid of the hissing dynamite, except to run out of the tomb and chance a long throw.

Then a dazed IQ stumbled over to him. Gritting his teeth, IQ grabbed the burning fuse between his thumb and forefinger and pulled. The fuse popped out, and he dropped it on the floor and stomped on it. The tomb was dark again.

'What a bright idea,' James said in relief.

He made his way outside and blinked in the sunlight. In the distance he could see the two robbers tearing off into the valley. His friends and the Professor joined him.

'They seem remarkably fit for having been sealed inside a three-thousand-year-old tomb,' the Professor observed.

'Yes,' James agreed wryly. 'It must be the dry desert air.'

IQ moved over to James and held out a small black shape. James took it and looked at it closely. It was a scarab, a stone cut into the shape of a beetle. On its back were the same hieroglyphs he'd seen on the hilt of the knife from the boat.

'Interesting,' he said. 'Where did you get this?'

'I knocked it off the lapel of the thug who grabbed the Professor and me,' IQ explained.

As James slipped it into his pocket he heard loud voices. Nearby, Gordo was trying to help Cleo to her feet. Angrily, she brushed him aside and stood up unaided.

'I do not need you to get back to my feet,' she snapped. Through the veil of the *chador* only her eyes could be seen. They looked like they could start a fire. 'I need nothing from foreigners like you.'

'Whoa, major attitude,' Gordo complained,

joining his friends. 'So, who were those dudes? And where'd they come from?'

James shook his head. 'I'm not sure, Gordo. They were inside the tomb *before the seal was broken*. Maybe we'll discover how they got in there when we explore it further.'

Professor Gheeza turned back to the tomb. 'It's late now,' he said. 'All this excitement has been a bit much for me. We'd better close the tomb for tonight and begin our excavation tomorrow morning.'

James and Gordo helped him push the heavy door closed. Then the Professor turned to Farid. 'You'd better get two men you can trust,' he said. 'Have them stand guard through the night. No one is to enter – or leave – the tomb until then.'

'Leave!' James said, smacking his forehead. 'I just remembered – Trevor's still in there.'

Gordo shrugged. 'So let him stay there.'

'It's tempting,' James replied with a smile. 'After all, he's no more in the dark than usual. But we can't do it.'

'No,' Tracy agreed reluctantly. 'I guess we can't. Although he's such a jerk, I wish we could.'

Professor Gheeza couldn't hold back a smile. 'There's a word for people like him, a word that has been passed down from generation to generation from time unknown.'

'What's that?' Tracy asked.

'We call them *pyramidiots*.'

CHAPTER 6

The Secret of the Scarab

'Doesn't the Nile look beautiful at night, Mr Milbanks?' James asked, gazing out at the river. In its dark waters he could see the reflection of the large, full moon. Also mirrored in the water was the flashing neon sign of the Nile Hotel, where they were staying. Despite this, the view was quite spectacular.

The headmaster ignored the view and glared angrily at James. 'Don't change the subject on me, Bond.' Professor Gheeza had felt it his duty to tell him about the attack at the tomb. As usual, at the first hint of trouble Mr Milbanks laid down the rules. Over and over again.

'You and this entire group are here as guests of Cairo University, remember?' he growled. 'I agreed to this expedition because I thought it would be educational. Now you make me wonder if I made the right decision. Fights inside a tomb! Explosives thrown at my daughter! One more stunt like this and I shall cancel the rest of this field trip.'

'But sir,' Phoebe said from the other end of

the room, 'they need our help on this dig. You'd really be letting them down if you pulled us out now.' She was standing with Gordo, Tracy, and IQ. They were all doing their very best to look apologetic and innocent. Trevor was standing off by himself, hardly able to keep the smirk off his face. He loved seeing James getting a talking to.

'Don't think I'm not aware of it,' Mr Milbanks replied. 'It's the only reason I haven't sent you home yet. But you're here to help *uncover* the past – not destroy it! Or yourselves!'

Trevor smiled brightly and held up his hand. 'I have an idea, sir,' he said.

Gordo groaned. 'Like, we're not in class, bonehead.' Rudely, he mimicked Trevor raising his hand.

Ignoring him, Trevor continued. 'Why not just send Bond home and let the rest of us stay?'

'Trevor, you worm,' Phoebe muttered.

Tracy stepped towards her father. 'But Daddy,' she said calmly, 'James was just trying to –'

James held up his hand, stopping her in midsentence. 'It's all right, Tracy. I agree with your father.' He turned to the headmaster. 'I promise you, sir, that I'll be on my best behaviour from this moment on.'

Mr Milbanks stared at him as if expecting a trick. Then he coughed. 'Well, see that you

31

are.' He sighed and shook his head. 'I'm glad I thought to pack my Walkman. What I need now is some nice, restful Beethoven.' Knowing the coast would now be clear for hours, everyone heaved sighs of relief. Trevor slunk back to his room.

Tracy turned to James as soon as her father had left the room. 'Why did you stop me from telling him about the tomb robbers?'

'Because he'd turn things over to the police. And then they'd seal off the tomb. The Professor's work would be delayed for who knows how long. And there's no guarantee they'd catch anyone.' James stared out over the Nile again. 'But if we investigate ourselves, then we may be able to work out what's going on. Once we find enough out, *then* we'll tell your father.'

'But we don't know anything yet,' Gordo said, flicking a date into his mouth from a bowl on a nearby table.

'Yes, we do,' IQ broke in. 'I managed to get a telephone line hooked into my laptop. I cracked the police files and searched for information on that knife James found.'

'And?' Tracy asked excitedly.

'The hieroglyphs are a gang marking,' IQ said. 'They've been found on the equipment used by the men of someone called Pharaoh Fearo.'

'Who?' Phoebe looked puzzled.

'That *I* can tell you,' Cleo said from the

32

doorway. She still wore the red, floor-length dress and veil. 'He's a monster, a maniac who is convinced he's a true descendant of the pharaohs who once ruled our country. He has committed many atrocities, including robbing museums of their treasures and selling them to foreigners, to people like you who come here to loot our land.'

'We aren't the ones robbing tombs,' James pointed out. 'We're just trying to help.'

'Help yourselves, you mean,' Cleo snapped.

'Give it up, James,' Tracy suggested. She glared at Cleo. 'Some people won't listen because of their own prejudices. *We're* not her enemies, but she refuses to see that.'

Cleo turned to her. 'For thousands of years, foreigners have stolen the treasures of my country. Until I have reason to trust you, I think I am only wise to suspect your every action.' Then, with a slight incline of her head, she swept out of the room.

'Talk about personality problems!' Phoebe said.

'She just has strong opinions,' James replied. 'Sooner or later she'll realize she's wrong.'

'I'll vote for later,' Gordo said. He'd finished off the dates and had started on a bowl of figs.

James took the scarab IQ had given him out of his pocket and held it under the light on the table. It seemed to be made from a single piece of solid stone. But it felt awfully light. Could it be hollow?

He took out his pocket-knife and opened the

33

blade. Using the point, he probed for a joint. With a grin, he inserted the blade into a thin crack in the beetle's back and then prised the top off the figure.

Inside was a small compartment filled with a tissue-thin paper folded into a tiny wad. James pulled it out and dropped the scarab to the table. He unfolded the sheet of paper and spread it out on the table.

It was a map. The coast of Egypt, the course of the Nile, and the outline of the Arabian peninsula were all obvious. But there were several dotted red lines that joined spots in Saudi, marked by circles, to spots in Egypt.

'It's a map of the region,' Tracy said, puzzled. 'But what are those lines and circles?'

IQ and Phoebe came over to look, too. Gordo yawned and went on eating.

'I'm not sure,' James replied to Tracy's question. Then he tapped the southernmost of the circles in Egypt. It lay on a bend in the Nile. 'But I'll bet this one is Luxor.'

Catching on, IQ grinned. 'Maybe even the tomb of Amenhotep I?'

'Right.' James handed him the paper. 'Maybe you can go over this,' he suggested. 'See if you can figure out what the circles might be. And what the dotted lines mean.'

'If what Cleo says about this Pharaoh Fearo is true, no doubt he's up to something illegal,' Tracy put in. 'Who knows, maybe he's trying to take over the world or something.'

'Whatever he's up to, we've got to stop him,' James said. 'There have been three attempts to kill Professor Gheeza already. It doesn't seem likely that Pharaoh Fearo will stop now. From here on in, we'd better keep a sharp lookout. And we'd better keep on our toes, too.'

Gordo suddenly shot to his feet, holding one hand over his mouth. 'Yo! Get out of my way!' he yelled, charging from the room.

Phoebe blinked. 'Talk about on your toes. Has someone poisoned the fruit?'

IQ shook his head. 'Nothing like that,' he said. 'But I think Gordo just found out what happens when you're a fig pig.'

CHAPTER 7

Ready for Action

In the morning, James and the others were to meet Professor Gheeza at the tomb. After what had already happened, James wanted to be ready for anything. He checked to see that his watch was fully charged. Not only did it tell the time, but IQ had improved it by adding a few extras to help James whenever he got into trouble – which was often. A small buzz-saw, a miniature laser, and even four tiny missiles were contained in the watch and could be operated by various buttons around the watch's rim.

As James was preparing there was a knock at the door. IQ entered without waiting for James's reply. Once he was in the room, he removed two ordinary-looking water flasks from the backpack he carried. They were made of metal, and had flat bottoms to allow them to stand up. IQ strapped one of the flasks to James's belt and grinned at his friend's surprised look.

'It seems quite ordinary, doesn't it?' he asked. Then he raised the second flask gripped the cap. 'But if you twist the cap in the wrong direction, it releases a capsule.' He demon-

36

strated. With a grating sound, the cap spun clockwise. James heard a fizzing sound. IQ quickly set the flask down on James's desk. 'The contents are now the most powerful acid known to man.'

As he said this he pointed. James saw that the flask was smoking. Then rust-coloured patches appeared on its surface. After a few seconds, these patches split apart and a hissing steaming liquid spilled onto the desk. The flask dissolved, and the acid ate through the wood of the desk and flowed onto the floor. Loud hissing filled the room as the acid began to eat through the floor. It ran out of steam milli-metres from burning straight through to the room below.

James raised an eyebrow. 'I've heard of acid rain, but the people in the room below nearly got an acid shower!' He eyed the flask strapped to his belt. 'And what do I do if I get thirsty?'

IQ shrugged. 'Look for a drinks machine, I guess.'

'Wonderful.' James strapped his real flask on his belt and marked it with a pen so he'd be sure to drink from the right one. 'Do you have any more useful inventions?' James asked.

'I didn't bring along many of them,' IQ said. 'Just the ones I thought might come in handy on a dig, I'm afraid. I had no idea we'd be running into this nasty Pharaoh Fearo.' He dug into his pack and pulled out what looked like an ordinary flashlight. 'A carbon arc lamp,' he said. 'This tiny device has the same illuminating power of an airport searchlight.'

'Ah. You're travelling light,' James commented.

'And *this*,' IQ continued, removing a folded shovel from his backpack, 'is my sonic shovel.'

James looked at it with interest. 'What does it do? Play music while you dig?'

'No, nothing like that,' IQ said, unfolding the shovel. There were several buttons on the handle and a couple of dials. 'The blade vibrates and gives off low-pitched sounds that make whatever you're digging through easier to move. The shovel goes through soil like a hot knife through butter. It's a new invention, and I thought I'd try it out while we're here.'

'It sounds great, IQ,' James agreed. 'But I doubt that Professor Gheeza will let you dig with it too close to the tomb.'

'True. The vibration it generates might harm an ancient structure.' IQ laid it on the remains of James's desk. 'I guess I'll leave it here for the time being.'

James glanced at his watch. 'Speaking of time, we'd better head down and join the Professor. We don't want to hold him up.' He and IQ hurried out of the room.

A moment after they had left, the door opened and Trevor slipped inside. He headed for the desk and picked up the shovel. With a smile, he packed it into his own backpack. He had been eavesdropping outside the door and heard everything that IQ said.

'Maybe you and the others are here for the scientific aspect of this trip,' he muttered. 'But I believe that a little digging on the side might turn up a few artefacts that may make this trip worthwhile for me. They'd be worth a fortune back home in England . . .'

When the excavation party arrived at the tomb, James saw with approval that the guards Farid had posted the previous night were still on duty. After checking with them, Farid reported that there had been no further signs of robbers. And no mysterious underground rumblings.

'Good,' Professor Gheeza said. Rubbing his hands together, he turned to look over the rest of the party. Tracy, Phoebe, Gordo, and IQ were all with James. Trevor stood slightly apart, and Cleo – still in her all-enveloping robe and veil – watched everyone like a hawk. She clearly didn't trust them. The Professor gestured for them all to gather around so he could explain the day's activities to them.

'Farid will be using the camera to record every artefact we find,' he told them. 'It is important to note meticulously where each is situated in the tomb. The placement can tell us a lot about the culture of the ancient Egyptians.' He gestured to the tables and supplies. 'Everything we might need is here. Now, I know you probably all think that this is going to be very exciting, that we'll just pull the treasures out as we find them. But we cannot work like that. Every effort must be made to ensure that all the facts about our findings are carefully recorded. It is painstaking work, and very slow.'

'Bummer,' Gordo muttered. 'It'll take forever to get to the mummy at this rate.'

'It may well take a few weeks,' the Professor agreed. 'But this is all vital work and cannot be rushed. Now follow me.'

James held back as the Professor entered the tomb so he could talk to IQ and Tracy alone. 'I know that the Professor thinks this is going to be a normal excavation,' he said. 'But I doubt that Pharaoh Fearo has been trying to kill him just to stop the news of this tomb getting out. We'd better stay extra alert in there.'

Cleo was staring at them suspiciously from the entrance to the tomb. When James, IQ, and Tracy joined the others, Cleo tagged along just behind James. Somehow, though, James didn't think it was because she found him irresistible. More likely she was watching to make sure he didn't steal anything.

The passageway led down into the cool earth. The heat of the desert above was soon left behind. The Professor and Farid both carried lights, and IQ had his flashlight on low power so they could all see in the cramped tunnel. As the Professor reached the first of the artefacts on the floor, he stopped. Carefully, he shone his light ahead of them.

The tunnel continued another six feet or so, then ended in a second sealed door. Between them and the door lay the scattered objects James and the others had seen the previous day. On either side of the door were two large wooden statues. Both were of human figures with jackal's heads, and each was carrying a long staff. The paint on the statues was as bright and clear as if it had been painted only a few weeks earlier.

'Anubis, guardian of the dead,' James murmured. Cleo seemed surprised he knew anything at all about ancient Egyptian religion.

Tracy grinned. 'I've been out with a couple of guys who looked like that,' she joked.

The Professor called back over his shoulders, 'Beyond this door will lie the real treasure room, and beyond – with luck – the burial chamber. In there, I hope, will lie the mummy of Amenhotep I.'

Cleo's eyes showed her happiness at this thought. 'He has lain there undisturbed for thousands of years. Since 1493 B.C.'

James had been using his own flashlight to look over the wall carvings. Most showed the pharaoh with various animal-headed Egyptian gods. But one of them showed the king with his wife. The artist had caught all of the beauty and life of the long-dead queen.

'Superb workmanship,' he commented. 'As fine as the carving of Queen Nefertiti also discovered near here.'

'What do you know of Nefertiti?' Cleo asked scornfully.

'Not much,' James replied. 'She was the wife of Akhnaton and the mother-in-law of King Tut. An excellent sculpture of her head was found in the ruins of a sculptor's workshop. It's now in a Berlin museum.'

Cleo's gaze was now more thoughtful than hostile. 'Perhaps I have judged you too quickly. Not many foreigners know much about Egypt's past.'

'I'm also interested in Egypt's present,' James replied. 'Perhaps you could fill me in a little more some evening – say, over dinner?'

Her eyes remained expressionless at this. 'You are quite persistent,' she said.

As James opened his mouth to respond the floor of the passageway began to vibrate. Uneasily, they looked around. The smaller statues were starting to wobble where they stood. Professor Gheeza's eyes filled with fear.

'An earthquake!' he shouted. 'This could bring down the roof and destroy all of these treasures!' He hesitated, clearly torn between his duty as a scientist and his instincts as a man concerned with saving the past. As a scientist, he knew he was not supposed to move anything without photographing its original placement. But he also knew that if he didn't begin moving the objects *now*, they might all be destroyed.

'I don't think it's an earthquake,' IQ yelled over the rumblings. 'It feels all wrong.'

'It feels scary enough to me!' Trevor yelled. He turned and ran for the exit.

Then the noise and vibration died as suddenly as they had begun.

'Quiet as a tomb in here now,' Gordo said with a grin.

'That was some weird earthquake,' Phoebe noted.

'If that was an earthquake, I'll eat my hat, pith and all,' IQ said firmly.

'Shhhh!' James held up his hand for silence. For a moment all they could hear was the sound of their own breathing.

Then, from beyond the sealed door, there came scraping noises. James felt the hair on the back of his neck start to rise. No one had entered the other room in over three thousand years! All that should be inside was the pharaoh's mummy – and that should definitely not be moving around!

CHAPTER 8

I Want My Mummy
. . . Not!

'I think,' James said softly, 'that it's time to forget the scientific approach, Professor.' He pointed at the sealed stone door. 'We'd better get inside there and see what's making those sounds.'

'I'm not sure I really want to know,' Phoebe said, shivering.

'What else can we do?' Tracy asked her. 'Knock and see if anyone's home?'

'Well, why don't we just come back later?' Phoebe suggested hopefully.

'Because there may not be anything to come back to later,' James explained. 'If Pharaoh Fearo is around, then there's a perfectly good explanation for what caused that noise inside the tomb – his men, looting it. The only thing I can't explain is how they got in there.'

The Professor nodded in agreement. 'Whatever is going on here,' he said, 'I'm afraid we cannot wait to investigate it later.' He turned to his assistant. 'Farid, be careful to photograph everything as we work. We need as much of this recorded as we can.' Then he looked at James. 'Well, let's go ahead and open the inner door.'

Carefully they made their way to the door. When they reached the solid slab of stone blocking the way, the Professor removed his hammer and chisel from the small tool pack at his waist. Once Farid had snapped a picture of the seal, a single blow from the hammer shattered it.

'All right, Gordo,' James said with a grin, 'do your thing.'

'No problemo!' Gordo put his back to the door and heaved with all his might. His muscles bulged, and he grunted once.

The door swung open as smoothly and easily as if it had been oiled.

As the Professor and IQ shone their torches into the room beyond, everyone gasped in astonishment. Everywhere the beams touched there was the glitter of gold. There were gold statues, gold tables and chairs, and gold spears. There were jewelled chests and golden goblets. There was even a golden game board with gold game pieces. The room seemed to be overflowing with sparkling metal and precious gems.

The tomb was about ten feet wide by ten feet long and eight feet high. The walls and ceiling were covered with carvings and paintings. At the far end of the room was an arched doorway. On the left was what looked like a solid door, and on the right was a small alcove.

The Professor focused his beam on the left wall. 'Intriguing,' he announced. 'Either that is a fake door or it leads to another treasure room.'

'A fake door?' Tracy asked.

'The ancients were fond of them,' Cleo explained. 'They look real, but there is solid stone behind them. They can make the room look much bigger than it really is and therefore mislead robbers.'

Shining his light on the alcove, Professor Gheeza said, 'That's the *shabty* room, I should think.'

'It doesn't look that shabby to me,' Phoebe said.

'Not *shabby*,' Cleo corrected her. '*Shabty*. Those are small models of the pharaoh showing him doing all sorts of work. The ancients believed that after death the pharaoh had to do a number of jobs, so they made little likenesses of the king that were supposed to come to life to do the work for him.'

'Mondo bizarro,' Gordo said.

The Professor laughed and aimed his beam at the far doorway. 'And through there should lie the sarcophagus – the stone coffin – of Amenhotep I.'

James studied the layout of the room. Everything seemed to be very clean. There wasn't even any dust on the floor. He pointed this out to the Professor. 'Don't you think that after three thousand years it should be a little messy?'

'I'll say!' Tracy agreed. 'When I think how my room looks within minutes of cleaning . . .'

'If that's the burial chamber,' Gordo joked, 'maybe the king dude has a burial chamber-maid.'

James led the way slowly into the other room tiptoeing through the golden artefacts. He resisted the urge to pick one up to look at it. *How much must all of this gold be worth?* he wondered.

In the doorway to the burial chamber, he stopped and sent the beam of his flashlight into the other room. Cleo – who had remained close to him since they entered the tomb – gasped and clutched his arm.

In the centre of the small room was a huge slab of stone. James held his breath and crossed quietly to the sarcophagus. Cleo stood beside him, pointing to several of the hieroglyphs cut into the surface.

'That's the signet of Pharaoh Amenhotep I!' she cried, delighted. 'This must be where his mummy lies!'

'Untouched for three thousand years!' the Professor added.

'If no one's been in here in three thousand years,' James asked, 'then what caused that noise we heard?' He pointed at the stone coffin. 'I don't think the pharaoh's been throwing a party.'

IQ shone his light around the room. 'There

doesn't seem to be any more to this tomb,' he agreed. 'Just these two rooms. And there's no sign of anyone having been here before us.'

'Maybe it's haunted,' Phoebe suggested, glancing over her shoulder. 'Maybe it was a ghost we heard earlier, trying to warn us to stay away.'

'Nonsense,' IQ said firmly. 'There are no such things as ghosts. All that's in here is a very dead pharaoh.'

Gordo tried to lift the lid off the coffin. After a few tries he gave up. 'No way has he been popping in and out,' he said, wiping the sweat from his forehead. 'Somebody's kept the lid tight on him.'

Professor Gheeza smiled. 'I think we'll need a pulley and crane to remove that lid,' he said.

Tracy shivered as she looked around the small room. 'So what is going on in this place?'

'That's a good question,' James replied. 'I just hope we can come up with a good answer.'

'I'll be happy with any explanation you come up with, James,' Phoebe said, staring at him with a worried look. 'As long as it doesn't involve walking mummies.'

CHAPTER 9

Striking Oil

After eating dinner at the hotel, the gang from Warfield headed for James's room. This time, Cleo included herself in the party while Trevor disappeared off on his own. As usual, no one missed him.

Spreading the map that he had found in the scarab on the desk, James looked at IQ. 'Did you have any luck figuring this out?' he asked.

'I think so.' IQ tapped the marked circles on the Arabian peninsula. 'Each of these points indicates an oil field.'

'Oil?' Tracy asked. 'Then maybe these dotted lines are pipelines of some kind.'

'It doesn't make any sense to pipe oil from Saudi Arabia to Egypt,' Phoebe objected.

'Maybe it does,' James said, slowly. 'After all, if we're right and Pharaoh Fearo's involved, I doubt he's *buying* oil. What if he's stealing it? Through some kind of secret pipeline?'

Cleo shook her head. 'But the length of each pipeline involved would be well over a thousand miles! Surely there is no way he could possibly build a pipeline that long, let alone half a dozen of them.'

Giving her an approving smile, IQ nodded.

'It does seem highly unlikely,' he agreed. 'And besides, where could he build a refinery in Egypt that wouldn't be instantly observed? He'd have to find somewhere to hide it.'

James pointed to the map again. 'What about the marked spots in Egypt?' he asked. 'Could they be where he plans to build his refineries?'

'I don't think so,' IQ said. 'They all indicate ancient sites, like this one. He can't be planning to hide refineries inside tourist attractions, can he?'

'Not unless he's crazy,' James agreed. He shook his head, baffled. 'None of this makes any sense.'

Phoebe spoke up again. 'And what about the noises in the tomb today?' she asked. 'Was that Pharaoh Fearo's work, too?'

'The doors were sealed when we opened them,' Cleo said. 'Yet somehow two robbers got into the tomb. And *someone* – or something – was in the burial chamber earlier, but wasn't there when we broke through.'

'Maybe the place *is* haunted,' Phoebe said. 'There doesn't seem to be any other answer.'

'We don't have all the pieces of the puzzle yet,' James told her. 'I guess we just have to wait and see what happens tomorrow.' James wanted to be reassuring. But he could tell they were all wondering the same thing: was there really a *natural* explanation for what had happened in the tomb that afternoon?

*

51

The next morning, they approached the tomb with mixed feelings. Professor Gheeza seemed to be concerned only about his work. The problems of the previous day hadn't bothered him at all. And Farid looked as neutral as he always did. But James and his friends were tense and a little worried. What would happen next?

As they unloaded their gear from the old truck the two guards spoke quietly with Farid. Farid then reported to the Professor.

'It was a quiet night,' he said. 'Both men heard nothing and saw no one.'

'What about the third guard?' Cleo asked. 'Is he still inside the tomb?'

'I expect so,' the Professor replied. 'Let's go and tell him he can go home and get some breakfast now. Come along.' He led the group into the passageway. James and Cleo followed, James carrying his flashlight to light the way. The others filed in behind them.

The intense beam of light made the wall carvings look like they were coming to life. Yet the musty smell of centuries of decay was all about them. It was definitely a creepy place.

Professor Gheeza gave a startled cry and pointed into the burial chamber. The guard lay in a heap on the floor. He wasn't moving at all. James and Cleo rushed forward.

'Out cold,' James said, examining the man.

'Perhaps he fell asleep?' Cleo suggested.

'This isn't sleep,' James told her. 'There's a bump on the back of his head, and he doesn't look like he's ready to wake up. He was knocked out, and pretty recently, too.'

They looked at each other and then at the others, who had paused in the doorway to the treasure room.

'The coffin lid!' IQ cried. 'The hieroglyphs for the king's name were on the left-hand side yesterday.'

James stood up and inspected the lid. He remembered that, too. A cold feeling tingled down his spine as he studied the lid. The name of Amenhotep was now on the right-hand side of the coffin. The only way that could have happened was if the lid had been moved.

With a sudden scream, the guard sat upright. Wild-eyed, he looked around the room, shaking like a leaf. Farid grabbed the man and barked a question in Arabic. In a quavering voice, the man replied. Even in the poor light, James could see that Farid's face drained of blood. His hands were shaking as he let the guard go. The man instantly jumped to his feet and ran shrieking out of the room.

'I don't want to know!' Phoebe moaned. 'Whatever it is, I don't want to know.'

'The . . . the guard says that he heard a noise,' Farid said. 'He looked at the sarcophagus and the lid came off it. Then the mummy of Amenhotep rose from the crypt and attacked him!'

'That's completely impossible,' IQ said firmly. Then he looked at the faces of his friends and seemed to lose some of his confidence. 'Well, isn't it?'

James looked down at the lid of the coffin. That huge weight that even Gordo couldn't shift had somehow been turned around. The guard couldn't have done it. That left just one other possibility: it had somehow been opened from the *inside*.

CHAPTER 10

Earthquake!

With all of the excitement, no one had noticed that Trevor hadn't entered the tomb. Instead, he hung around the entrance until the others had gone in. Then, smiling to himself, he took IQ's sonic shovel from his backpack.

'The others can knock themselves out helping that old fool if they like,' he muttered. 'But I'm going to help myself to something to make this trip special.' He examined the shovel. 'Now, how do you turn this on? I'm certainly not going to work my fingers to the bone digging.' There were several controls on the handle. One was marked STRENGTH. 'I'll let this thing do the work,' he decided, setting it to FULL.

At that moment, the guard from inside the tomb ran out at full speed, yelling and screaming. He almost knocked Trevor over, and then headed off into the desert. Trevor glared after him, annoyed.

'Stupid time and place to go jogging,' he said to himself. 'No wonder he's all worked up.' He turned back to the shovel and found the on/off switch. Putting the blade of the shovel on the closest piece of ground, he switched it on.

The shovel sprang to life with the hum of an electric motor. There was a slight vibration in the handle but Trevor steadied himself and pressed down with the blade. It sliced straight through the ground with ease. 'Amazing!' he admitted. 'Maybe that twerp IQ does know what he's doing.'

Then the blade collided with the underlying rock. Unable to cut through solid stone as easily as sand and soil, the blade began to vibrate loudly. Trevor was impatient and he pushed down even harder. Leaning all of his weight on the handle, Trevor was able to sink the edge of the blade into the rock. Then the trouble really began.

The vibrating blade sent a shock wave through the ground as the shovel dug deeper. With a startled cry Trevor lost his footing and let go of the shovel. The ground was shaking below his feet and the sand was jumping into the air. Trevor fell down and was bounced about by the growing shudders in the rock.

Inside the tomb, James and Cleo were in the burial chamber trying to figure out what had happened to the coffin. The others had gone back to the treasure room to look at the artefacts.

Phoebe, looking scared, said, 'Maybe there really is a curse on this place.'

'Now, Phoebe,' IQ said patiently, 'there's no such thing as a curse. Nothing in here moves unless someone moves it.'

'Oh yeah?' Tracy said, pointing at the nearest statues. 'Look!'

The statues were bouncing up and down as the noise of the quaking earth filled the room. The floor started to vibrate under their feet, and dust and stones began to rain down from the ceiling.

'It's another earthquake!' Farid screamed, rushing back up the corridor to the outside. 'And worse than before!'

Professor Gheeza looked at all of the priceless relics in the tomb. He was afraid that if they left, the statues and everything else would be wrecked. But if they tried to save them, they might all be killed if the tunnel collapsed.

In the burial chamber, James and Cleo turned to get out of the tomb. They were just in time to see the far wall of the tomb breaking away from the rock. Then, as Cleo screamed, the wall started to collapse.

Without thinking, James grabbed Cleo and threw her down behind the stone sarcophagus. Then he dropped down beside her, trying to protect her from the debris flying around them. His mouth and nose filled with dust. With a blast of shattering stones, the wall collapsed on top of them.

In the treasure room, Tracy stared in horror as the roof in front of them bowed downwards, and then broke free in a shower of dust and boulders. The entrance to the burial chamber – where James and Cleo were – was rapidly filling up.

'James!' Tracy screamed, afraid he'd been killed by the blocks. She started forwards, but Gordo's strong arm whipped around her stomach and dragged her backwards. He was barely in time, as the roof ruptured all at once. In a thunder of rock, the burial chamber was sealed off completely.

'Chill, babe,' Gordo said between coughs. 'Let's make like a drum and beat it!'

'I've never known an earthquake to be so powerful!' Professor Gheeza yelled.

'I've never wanted to know one!' Phoebe screamed back.

The flying dust was almost blinding them. IQ was trying to clean off his glasses, but each time he wiped them more dust immediately settled on the lenses. He couldn't see anything.

Above ground, Trevor had managed to get to his feet again. Staggering from the vibrations, he tripped towards the shovel and started hitting all of the switches. 'Shut off, blast you!' Finally he hit the right switch and the shovel died.

He turned to the tomb, afraid that the others would rush out in a second and yell at him for causing such a disaster. But as he looked at the entrance, its supporting pillars cracked, shattered, and collapsed. In a roar, dust and smoke blew out of the tomb. When the air cleared, Trevor saw that the passageway was sealed off.

Everyone but Trevor was trapped in the crypt!

CHAPTER 11

The Only Way
out is in

Silence descended once again inside the tomb.
As James stood up dust and small pebbles fell
from his clothing. Amazingly, except for a few
bruises, he was unhurt. He helped Cleo to her
feet. She seemed to be fine, too. They had
been very lucky. In the light from his flashlight, James glanced through the dust-filled air,
coughing. They had been very lucky, except
for one thing.

The only exit from the room was completely
sealed off. The arch of the doorway had collapsed during the earthquake and so had the
ceiling.

'James?' Through the pile of rocks, he could
barely make out Tracy's faint voice. 'James?
Are you all right?'

He leaned over the rubble, being careful not
to knock any more rocks loose. 'We're okay!'
he called back. 'Though it looks like the day's
off to a rocky start. Is everybody else all
right?'

Tracy looked around the treasure room.
One lens of IQ's glasses was cracked, and

they all had a few cuts and bruises. Their clothing was filthy, and there was dust in their hair. But IQ's strong flashlight was still illuminating the room.

'We're fine!' she yelled back.

'Yeah,' Phoebe grunted. 'We're thinking of holding a picnic in here.'

IQ leaned over the rocks, cupping his hands to his mouth. 'It looks as if we're sealed in here.'

Professor Gheeza coughed and then sniffed. 'It's already starting to get a little stuffy,' he commented. 'We are in grave danger of running out of oxygen.'

James heard the Professor's warning. He knew that he and Cleo faced the same peril, and probably before the others, since the burial chamber was much smaller than the treasure room. The air already felt thick and it was beginning to get hot.

Before he could say anything, Cleo pointed at the stone coffin and called, 'James! Look!'

The lid had twisted slightly in the quake and now lay at a slight angle. Inside the sarcophagus, there was the faint glint of metal.

James grabbed the edge of the lid, and with Cleo's help he managed to raise it a few inches. To their surprise, it moved smoothly and without a sound. And when they let go, it stayed in position. James pointed the light into the coffin and they both gasped.

Except for a pair of slightly twisted metal

supports that held the lid in place, the coffin was completely empty. James pulled out his penknife and scraped the lid. The stone covering chipped away to reveal a metal case underneath.

'It's a fake,' Cleo said, puzzled. 'But why is it so heavy? Gordo couldn't even budge it.'

James gave her a grin. 'Not because of the weight.' He pointed to a small box inside the lip of the stone coffin. 'A magnetic lock clamped the lid on. It must have shifted during the earthquake and loosened the lid.' He bent to examine the interior of the coffin more closely 'And here's an infra-red eye,' he pointed out. 'It must open the lid from the inside.'

'But whatever for?' Cleo asked. 'I mean, a real mummy wouldn't need all of these gadgets.'

'No,' James agreed. 'But a fake one would.' It suddenly made perfect sense. 'You know, I think we've found the hidden way into this tomb!'

Cleo followed his gaze and smiled. 'And a way in can become a way out!' she said excitedly.

'Right.' James turned back to the doorway. 'Hang on!' he called to his friends. 'It looks like there's another way out of here. We'll get out and go for help!' He ignored their puzzled yells and turned back to Cleo. 'Well, I never thought I'd want to get into a coffin while I was still alive,' he told her. 'Are you ready?'

'In a moment,' she replied. 'I'm not exactly dressed for scrambling around, am I?' She gestured to her long *chador*. Then she unfastened her veil and threw back the hood of her robe. Undoing the robe, she stepped out of it. Underneath, she wore a faded pair of jeans and a neat white blouse.

Seeing the expression on James's face, she laughed. 'You didn't think I wore that stuff all of the time, did you?'

'Well, yes,' James admitted. 'You were very convincing about not showing yourself to strangers.'

She nodded. 'But you can't do the work of an archaeologist dressed like that. This is much more practical,' she said. 'Besides ...' She gave him a smile. 'I think I misjudged you earlier. You and your friends are not my enemies.' She held out her hand. 'Can we be friends?'

James shook her hand. 'With pleasure.'

'Good. Now let's find a way out of here.' She turned her attention back to the stone crypt. In one quick move, she sat on the edge of the sarcophagus and spun around so that she had her feet inside the coffin. James joined her. They looked at each other and then jumped in.

With their weight on it, the bottom fell out of the coffin. They dropped into a narrow, steep chute leading into the earth. James managed to hang onto his flashlight as they plummeted swiftly down the slide. He shone the light ahead of them and saw that they were flying directly towards a solid stone wall.

At the last second, part of the wall opened like a drawbridge. They slid to a gradual halt just beside the opening. In front of them was a room that looked like something out of a Hollywood movie. It seemed completely out of place several hundred feet below the desert sands. James and Cleo climbed slowly to their feet, staring around in wonder.

By the light of burning torches set in the walls, they could see that the room was almost a hundred feet long and at least thirty feet wide. Two rows of tall pillars supported the ceiling, which was covered with more carved scenes of ancient Egyptian life. On the floor were thick, luxurious carpets that were definitely not ancient.

Facing James and Cleo were six tall men in short, white skirt-like uniforms and sandals. Their chests were bare and they wore hoods on their heads. Each of them held a long sword, the points of which were at James's and Cleo's throats.

'Sorry,' James joked, 'I meant to call first, but I couldn't find a phone.'

'Bring the intruders here,' said a cold voice from the far end of the room.

One of the guards gestured with his sword, almost cutting off James's ear.

'That's what they call an offer you can't

refuse,' James said to Cleo with a tight smile. The guards fell in around them and they were led down the long room between the pillars.

Ahead of them was a raised stone platform, which held a large throne covered with gold and precious stones. A tall, musclebound man with a beard was sitting on the throne. He was dressed like the guards, except his head-dress and skirt were a deep royal blue. He had thick gold bands around his wrists and neck, and a gold ring held his hood in place. The ring was moulded in the shape of a cobra and had two fiery diamonds for eyes.

'Is it Halloween already?' James asked drily.

The man leaned forward. In one hand he held a golden whip; in the other, a small cane that looked like a shepherd's crook. He stared at James and then at Cleo. 'You are strangers in my country,' he said icily. 'So I will over-look your rudeness – this time. I am Pharaoh Fearo.'

'Your country?' James asked, looking around the room. 'Just what *is* your country, Pharaoh?'

'This is,' he replied, waving his hands.

'The whole room?'

The Pharaoh's eyes glittered dangerously. 'You are trying to provoke my anger. That is not very wise. Do not count on me being merci-ful towards you. I maintain my rule through strength and ruthlessness.' Then he stood up.

'Still, I can admire courage, and you have shown a good deal to get this far. You must be the young man who my agents tell me stopped them from killing that old fool, Professor Gheeza.'

'My name's Bond. James Bond Jr.'

'Ah.' The Pharaoh smiled. 'I have heard a little about you, then, from some . . . business associates of mine.' He looked at Cleo. 'And you must be Gheeza's student, Cleo Daway.'

'How do you know that?' Cleo asked.

'My dear, I am no fool.' The Pharaoh snapped his fingers. 'I have had the Professor under watch ever since he started his foolish excavations of my ancestor's tomb.'

Farid stepped out from behind one of the pillars. He bowed to the Pharaoh and knelt at his feet. 'There are still many who would rather serve the rightful pharaoh than the usurpers who rule in Cairo,' Fearo said. He waved Farid away. 'But you asked about my kingdom, didn't you, Bond? Well, it would please me to show it to you.'

'Could we do that later?' James asked. 'I was actually on my way to get help for the Professor and my other friends. They're trapped in the tomb above us.'

'Really?' The Pharaoh sounded bored. 'Well, they picked the right place to die, didn't they? Now, I offer you a choice. Either die right here, right now . . .' He snapped his fingers and the guards swung their swords into place at the throats of the two captives '. . . or come with me to see my realm – and then die.'

'I notice there's a lot of stress on dying,' James said.

Pharaoh Fearo smiled, nastily. 'Well, you know that the ancient Egyptians had a great deal of interest in death. I'm just following their example.'

'In which case, we'll follow you,' said James.

'Excellent.' The Pharaoh led the way out of the throne room. 'Now, come and behold my kingdom!'

CHAPTER 12

Into the Underworld

James and Cleo walked behind Pharaoh Fearo, the swords of the guards never far from their necks. Escape was impossible.

Fearo stopped in front of a large block of marble. It had a picture of his face carved into it. Burning torches lit the portrait from both sides. The Pharaoh held out his hand. 'The entrance to my realm!'

'Through a picture of yourself?' Cleo asked. 'You're not very modest, are you?'

'Modesty is for mortals, my dear,' the Pharaoh replied. 'As the true monarch of Egypt, I am a divine being.'

Cleo shot James a look but said nothing. Clearly, they were dealing with a madman.

Fearo went to the picture and pulled down on one of the torches. With a creak the block of stone spun open, revealing a short passage-way. The Pharaoh stepped aside, and the guards pushed James and Cleo into the tunnel. James could hear lapping water as they moved slowly through the darkness. The short walk ended in a huge natural cavern lit by hundreds of torches.

The cave was immense and had long, rocky

stalactites hanging from the roof, like giant fangs. The ground was perfectly level. Through the centre of the cave ran a small river. A small submarine floated on the surface.

'So that's how you attacked our boat,' James said. 'This river must lead to the Nile.'

The Pharaoh smiled coldly. 'An ancient water-way, dug thousands of years ago, known only to myself and my loyal subjects. Convenient, don't you think?'

James shrugged. 'All rats like holes in the ground.'

Fearo shuddered, but he managed to control his anger. 'I'll excuse your foolish comments for now,' he said. 'After all, you probably think I'm nothing but a common criminal.'

'Hardly a common one,' James answered.

'And not a criminal, either,' the mad king told him.

He led them along one wall of the cavern. James could make out tyre tracks on the ground. The air smelled of oil and machinery. Rounding a massive boulder, they found them-selves staring at a large, carved gateway. It was cut deeply into the wall of the cave and was at least as high and as wide as a house. Two huge stone statues of Fearo flanked the gateway.

'All true rulers of Egypt build their own temples,' the Pharaoh said proudly. 'My temple is not to some old god. Mine is to technology.'

Despite his dislike of their captor, James had to admit that the temple was impressive. It must have taken the madman years to build. But why had he carved it into solid rock? And why so far underground?

As they came closer to the entrance James could see that inside the gateway was a platform. Beside the platform was some kind of machine. It looked like one of the ancient reed boats in the scenes carved inside the tomb. On top of the craft was a small cabin with rows of portholes lining its sides. This was where the Pharaoh was leading them.

As they drew closer to this strange ship Cleo gasped, 'It's . . . it's covered with gold and jewels!' she exclaimed.

'Of course it is,' Fearo replied. 'Did you think that my chariot would be made of plain old *steel*?' He stopped at a ladder that led to a hatchway in the cabin and gestured at the craft. 'This is the world's first underground warship. A subterranean tunnelling machine that I have named the *Seth* – after the ancient god of disorder and the underworld.' He bounded up the steps and disappeared into the machine. The guards gestured with their swords for James and Cleo to follow.

The inside was just as fancy as the outside. The room James and Cleo stood in was filled with panels and computer screens. The seats at the controls were cushioned in red velvet, and there were gold statues of pharaohs and

gods all around the room. Several of the levers that controlled the *Seth* had jewelled knobs.

The guards followed them into the *Seth* and then sealed the exit. Fearo nodded with satisfaction and signalled the pilot who sat at the controls. 'Begin the journey,' he ordered.

The man set to work. James heard the distant whine of powerful motors, and the lights flickered on and off.

'Drills to full power,' the pilot ordered. 'Retract the protective cones.'

Fearo turned to his captives, a happy smile on his face. 'I always like this bit,' he said. 'It's so impressive.'

'Engage!' the pilot called.

The engines purred more loudly, and James could hear the whining of the drills. Then the *Seth* gave a shudder and the drills bit into the rock and sand. With a grinding noise, the ship surged forward into the earth.

James turned to the Pharaoh. 'It's all very nice,' he said. 'But it seems a bit boring to me.'

'Oh, very witty,' Fearo sneered. 'You'd better enjoy this trip, Bond – it's the last one you'll ever take.'

'I prefer sightseeing tours,' James replied. 'And there isn't too much to see down here.' He pointed to the portholes, which were covered by the soil and debris sliding past the ship.

'Then I'll tell you a story instead,' Pharaoh Fearo promised. 'Come to my quarters.'

There was a large gold throne in the next room, and Fearo immediately sat down in it. A man dressed in white brought him a golden cup filled with red liquid. Fearo took a small sip and sighed with pleasure. Suddenly two guards came up behind James and Cleo. In seconds, James and Cleo found their hands tied together. Then the servant and guards left. James and Cleo were now alone in the room with the Pharaoh. And completely helpless.

'Actually, I was rather pleased when you . . . uh, dropped in,' Fearo told James. 'I had expected to have to wait in my temple until I had killed that old fool Gheeza and resealed the tomb of Amenhotep I. But since he's trapped and will soon die from the lack of air, I can get on with my plan.'

'Why did you want to kill the Professor?' James asked calmly. He tried not to let his concern for his friends show.

'Because Fearo's a thief!' Cleo interrupted angrily. 'He wants to keep all of the treasure from the tomb of Amenhotep I for himself! He has stolen priceless treasures from his own people!'

'Stolen?' For the first time since they had met him, the Pharaoh looked really angry. 'I have stolen *nothing!* I am the rightful heir to the throne of Upper and Lower Egypt. All of its treasures belong to me!' He turned to a small chest beside his throne and took out a fat roll of parchment. 'I have my family tree to prove my claim! But the fools, the pretenders who run this country, refuse to acknowledge me. They want to keep Egypt for themselves. So now I must take it by force!' He glared down at his captives for a moment and then cracked a smile. 'I shall finish them off as I aim to dispose of you. Think about how foolish it was to challenge me – and wait for your terrible deaths!' He turned and strode out of the room, leaving James and Cleo tied together.

'James,' Cleo whispered, 'he's completely mad.'

'I'm glad you noticed,' James said softly.

'We have to stop him,' she added. 'But how? We're trapped! Now we and our friends may die! And this madman will destroy my country!'

CHAPTER 13

The Mummy Walks

Inside the treasure room of Amenhotep's tomb, the air was getting warm and thick. IQ took off his glasses, wiped the sweat from the lenses, and put them back on. They instantly fogged over again.

'Time's running out,' he said.

The others looked at him with gloomy expressions. Tracy and Phoebe looked terrible. Their hair was damp and plastered to their heads. Gordo was panting from the heat. And Professor Gheeza seemed to be on the verge of passing out. They were all sitting still with their backs against the wall. In order to save air they were trying not to move or talk too much.

'Bummer,' Gordo muttered.

'James will get help to us,' Tracy said firmly.

'I fear it will do little good,' the Professor said, sighing. 'A lot of rock fell in the entrance passage. It would take them hours to dig through to us.' He didn't have to bother adding, *And we don't have hours of air left.* They all knew what he meant.

'They might be able to drill a small hole

through the rubble,' IQ suggested. 'To let some fresh air in. Although I'm not sure James isn't stuck in the same fix we are.'

'Hey!' Phoebe cried excitedly. 'Listen! I can hear something!'

They all fell silent and strained their ears. Phoebe was right. There was something making noise – but it didn't sound like workmen digging. It sounded like footsteps. Slow, heavy steps from the supposedly empty corridor!

'It . . . it must be the mummy!' Phoebe whispered, shaking.

'Nonsense!' IQ said. 'How many times do I have to tell you that there's no such thing as a – ' His mouth dropped open, and he pointed at the entrance. There, in the glow of the flashlight, they could see the shape of a man completely wrapped in decaying bandages. Strips of greyish material flapped as the creature walked slowly towards them. It turned its head in their direction. Bright yellow eyes glowed behind the layers of shredded fabric. It was the mummy!

Trevor shook with fear as he stared at the wreckage he had caused. The passageway had collapsed and he knew that somewhere inside that tomb the rest of the party was trapped. And it was his fault.

Even though Trevor wasn't the nicest person in the world, he wasn't really bad. He was selfish and a little stupid. He was rich and spoiled. And he disliked James – but not enough to want him dead.

'I've got to get help,' Trevor muttered to himself. He couldn't let the others die. But who could he go to for help?

Then he remembered the foreman that the Professor had hired. Farina, or something – Farid, that was it. He had run out of the tomb just before it collapsed. He'd help the others out. Trevor looked around. Where was Farid? Trevor could see for some distance down the valley, but there was no sign of the man.

It was weird that the foreman had disappeared from the excavation site, but Trevor didn't have time to worry about it. Glancing around, he saw lines of tourists at the tombs at the other end of the valley. Some of them would be able to speak English. He'd go and get them to give him a hand.

He set off across the rocky ground towards the closest of the tombs. Suddenly the ground he was standing on gave way. With a cry, Trevor found himself falling into the black depths of the earth.

IQ tried to think of a logical, scientific explanation for what he was seeing. He knew that a person who had died over three thousand years ago couldn't be walking around. But he couldn't deny that the creature staring at him from the passageway looked pretty real.

Gordo seemed to agree. 'Either that's a mummy,' he said in a quiet voice, 'or it's some dude who just had a mondo wicked accident.'

'Are we taking a vote on it?' Phoebe asked, her voice quaking. 'I know which I'll go for!'

'This is ridiculous,' Tracy said. She was trying to sound confident, but there was a quaver in her voice. 'It's got to be a trick of some kind.'

'Feel free to try and prove it,' Phoebe said, hiding behind Tracy. 'I'm behind you – *way* behind you!'

Professor Gheeza looked pale. 'We know the tomb is sealed off,' he pointed out. 'And there was no one in that corridor a moment ago . . .'

The mummy was watching them, but he wasn't moving any closer. IQ regained some of his courage. He staggered to his feet. 'I say we rush it,' he declared. 'There are five of us and only one of it.'

The mummy raised its arms and let out a long deep moan. Then it turned and disappeared back into the passageway.

IQ looked at the others. 'We've got to follow it.'

'I'm with you,' Tracy told him. Together they started forward. Gordo fell in with them and Phoebe reluctantly brought up the rear. Professor Gheeza was too weak to move. The four friends cautiously edged their way into the mouth of the passage. They could see the fallen rocks that blocked their exit. Other than that, the passageway was totally empty.

Phoebe looked sick. 'I knew it,' she groaned. 'We're going to suffocate and die – and we're being haunted by Amenhotep's mummy as well!'

CHAPTER 14

Making a Big Mis-Snake

As soon as Fearo left the room to check on his crew, James set to work. He managed to get one hand free of the ropes and activate the small buzz-saw inside IQ's watch. The whirring blade quickly sliced through the ropes. Carefully they tiptoed to the half-open door and slipped through it.

On the other side was another short corridor that led to a room filled with churning engines and thick pipes. Vats of steaming hot liquid lined the walls. Above the vats was an upper level that could be reached only by a catwalk. This level housed all of the controls.

James and Cleo went up and examined a large display panel. There was a video monitor showing the view through the nose of the *Seth*. They could see huge diamond-tipped blades slicing through the soil, pushing it back along the sides of the mechanical mole.

All the controls were labelled with hieroglyphs. James couldn't read them but Cleo could. 'James,' she said excitedly, 'I think I know what's happening here. Look.' She pointed at the screen. 'The ship is cutting in a straight line through the ground. It automatically extracts metals from the earth and processes them in those vats below. Then other pipes take the pure metal to the back of the machine, where it's ejected into the tunnel behind us and forms a lining.'

James hit a button next to the screen. The picture switched to a map almost identical to the one he'd found in the scarab. But on this map, the line joining Luxor to Saudi Arabia was lit up. And a flashing gold light indicated a point under the Red Sea. It was moving slowly towards the Arabian peninsula.

'That has to be us,' James said, pointing to the gold light. 'This machine must be very fast. We're burrowing under the Red Sea and laying a pipeline behind us. The Pharaoh is trying to steal oil!'

'He'll steal anything that's not nailed down,' Cleo answered. 'But isn't this a bit crazy, even for him?'

James nodded. 'He's absolutely nuts about being the rightful ruler of Egypt. He must think he can use the money from selling the looted treasures and the oil he'll steal to try and gain the throne he thinks is his.'

'Not *thinks*,' corrected Pharaoh Fearo's booming voice. '*Knows* is his!'

A grim-faced Fearo and his guards were at the entrance to the engine room. None of them looked very happy to see James and Cleo standing at the control panel. Fearo gestured, and the four guards started up the catwalk after James and Cleo.

James dived for the stairs, his hands grabbing hold of a pipe that ran along the ceiling. He swung his legs up, catching the first guard in the chest and sending him flying off the catwalk to the floor below.

The second guard ducked and struck out at James with his sword. James let go of the pipe and flew over the edge of the metal walk. He landed on his feet on the floor of the engine room. The guard's blow hit the pipe that James had been holding onto and the sword punctured the metal. A blast of steam shot out, scalding the guard's ugly face.

'He's really steamed up,' James muttered. Looking about, he saw a long staff lying between the furnaces. It was used to clean the pipes, but James had a better use for it. He grabbed it and ran under the stairs, where the last two guards were. He could see their legs through the gaps between the steps. James thrust the end of the rod up between one guard's feet. With a cry, the man tripped over and tumbled down the stairs.

'He seems to have fallen down on the job,' James observed.

The last guard made it to the catwalk and charged at Cleo. She decided not to wait for him to arrive. Instead, she grabbed the chair at the video station and swung it in a circle.

The legs hit the man in the arm, and his sword stabbed through the bottom of the chair. The blade stopped barely an inch from Cleo's nose. She let go of the chair and pushed it at the guard.

The guard, overbalanced by the extra weight, stumbled backwards. Cleo grabbed one of the gold statues that Fearo had placed all over the ship. With a smile, she hit the guard over the head. He collapsed to the metal floor with a grunt.

'A solid-gold punch,' she said happily. Then she gave a cry as Pharaoh Fearo grabbed her. He leered down at her and held up his other hand. In it he gripped a small black snake that hissed and writhed. Its fangs were exposed and droplets of venom hung on the fierce tips.

'Bond!' the Pharaoh yelled. 'I've got a little historical riddle for you. What did Cleopatra say when the snake bit her? Give up? "I guess I asped for that!"' He laughed at his own terrible joke. 'And I've got an asp of my own here – along with a modern-day Cleo. Can I interest you in surrendering?'

James knew that asps were fatally poisonous, and that Fearo was insane enough to do anything. He stepped out into the open. 'You win, Fearo. I can't fight two snakes at once.'

'A very wise decision,' the Pharaoh agreed. He watched as two of the battered guards grabbed James. The third took Cleo and dragged her over to where James was standing.

Fearo crossed to a small cage that sat on the control panel and dropped the asp inside it. It hissed and struck at him but hit the glass wall of the cage. 'It seems a little mad at missing its chance,' Fearo said with a laugh.

'*You* seem more than a little mad to me,' James replied.

'I *am* mad,' the Pharaoh agreed. 'At the two of you.' He smiled nastily at James. 'But I have the perfect solution to the problem you pose. Ancient kings used to get rid of people by boiling them in oil. I'm afraid I can't supply the boiling part, but there's plenty of oil to go around.' He turned to the video screen and studied the information there. 'In fact, we're almost under an oil field right now.'

He picked up a microphone. 'Main control room, take us up to within fifteen feet of the surface. Immediately!' He turned to face James and Cleo. There was an evil gleam in his eyes. 'We're going to toss you out into my pipeline – and then cut into the oil field. You'll be drowned in oil when it gushes through. A really inventive way to kill you, don't you think?'

'With oil?' James shrugged. 'It sounds pretty crude to me.'

'A joker to the end, eh?' Fearo remarked. 'Well you always were a slick customer.'

Cleo groaned. 'I think I'd rather die than hear any more of your awful jokes.'

Pharaoh Fearo smiled at her. 'Well, that's

85

one wish I can promise you will come true.' He signalled to his guards. 'Take them to the emergency hatch,' he ordered. 'And toss this rubbish out!'

A few minutes later, James and Cleo were thrust out of the hatchway. They fell to their knees on the still-warm metal. Ahead of them, they could see the *Seth* churning away. At any second, it would break through into the oil field and flood the pipeline with oil.

CHAPTER 15

Giving Fearo the Slip

The *Seth* had crossed under the Red Sea and
was now under part of Saudi Arabia. On the
surface, the desert was broken by a small oasis.
Camped out among the date palms, the lush
grass, and the cool shade was a small tribe of
Bedouins. At one time, the Bedouins had all
been nomads, wandering the sands from waterhole to waterhole. In modern times many of
them had settled into towns, but some still
preferred the wandering life.

One of these was Sheikh Hassan al-Aboud.
He was a strong man even though he was in
his sixties. He owned many oil fields and was
immensely rich. Most of the year he spent in
his ultra-modern offices in Jedda, but for three
months of the year, he went back to the old
ways. Well, *almost.*

In his tent, he took a can of cola from his
portable refrigerator and sat back to watch
his favourite TV show on his projection TV.
Thanks to his portable satellite dish he could
choose from hundreds of channels. He was all
in favour of the traditional way of life, but he
wasn't fanatical about it.

Suddenly, the ground started to shake. The

can was jarred out of his hand, and cola soaked the expensive carpet on the floor of his tent. The TV shuddered then the picture went black. Sheikh Hassan leapt to his feet. 'By the beard of the Prophet!' he yelled. 'I knew I should have bought a VCR!'

The ground was still shaking, and he staggered across his tent to the entrance. Before he reached it, the centre pole cracked. The entire structure fell in on him.

He struggled out from under the cloth and spat sand out of his mouth. Straightening his burnoose, he yelled, 'May a thousand camels wet on the creep who has done this to me!' Then he stopped and stared.

Something was coming out of the desert towards his oasis. It was throwing up a mound just like a mole. But to make a mound that size, the mole would have to be thirty feet long!

James and Cleo watched the back of the *Seth* as it roared away. How much longer did they have?

Cleo turned to James. 'I am sorry for all the terrible things I said about you and your friends,' she told him. 'I had always believed it was foreigners like you who robbed my people. But now I see that the worst spoiler of all is one of my own.'

'There are good and bad people in all nations, Cleo,' James said. 'And we can all find friends across borders, too.' Then he smiled grimly. 'Still, let's leave the apologies for later. Right now, we have other things to worry about.'

'But what can we do?' Cleo asked. 'In seconds that ship will cut into the oil deposits and we shall be washed away in a flood of crude oil.'

'And I don't have my umbrella with me,' James replied. 'So we'd better get inside.' He took the flask that IQ had fixed for him from his belt. 'There's just one bus out of here, so let's catch it.' With Cleo following closely behind him, he ran after the swiftly moving *Seth*.

'If the oil breaks through, we are running towards our death,' Cleo panted.

'It's a chance we'll have to take,' James puffed back, reaching the rear of the mechanical mole. He gripped the flask in his left hand and took the cap in his right hand, giving it a quick flip clockwise. With a grinding sound, the cap released the acid-forming chemicals into the water. Tossing it by the cap, James threw the already-dissolving flask against the rear wall of the *Seth*. Instantly, the acid ate a hole in the metal. The gap grew by the second, and was soon large enough for James to leap through. Cleo followed him, and they both landed back inside the ship.

'What did you have inside that flask?' Cleo asked in wonder.

'My favourite cola,' James joked. 'It's the real thing.'

At that second, a gurgling sound drowned out the roar of the *Seth*'s motors. Then, with a rushing noise, oil flowed over the outside of the ship and began to flood the tunnel behind them.

It also started to pour into the *Seth* through the gap created by the acid.

'Uh-oh,' Cleo said, pointing.

'It might be time to abandon ship,' James agreed. But for now we'd better get out of this room!'

With the oil already starting to creep up around their feet, James and Cleo splashed their way forward. They were in a small storage room. Luckily the door was unlocked, and they passed through the doorway and closed it behind them. They had moved into the engine room, where they had been captured earlier. Ahead was the Pharaoh's cabin and then the control deck. The deck would be crawling with guards. They needed another way out!

Oil had already filled the small storage room. Black, heavy liquid was oozing through the cracks in the doorway and a stench like that of petrol fouled the air.

'The door won't be able to stand the pressure for long,' Cleo warned.

'Then let's get up to the catwalk,' James decided. 'Fast!'

Finally the door burst open and a flood of oil swept into the engine room. It started to bubble as it seeped over the motors and furnaces that processed the metals scooped from the earth.

'James!' Cleo cried. 'If the oil gets any hotter, this room will turn into a fireball!'

'Well,' James replied, 'at least Fearo would be happy that we boiled in oil.'

As they climbed up to the second level more and more oil forced its way into the engine room. It could only be a matter of time before the ship went up in flames.

Pharaoh Fearo's plans were going perfectly. This was the first of the pipelines through which he'd steal the wealth of the Arabian countries. He knew that he'd be able to find buyers for his oil, as well as for the ancient gold he had already stolen. Now that Bond and his silly friends were out of the way, nothing could ruin his plans. Soon he'd be swimming in money! Soon he'd –

The harsh shrill of an alarm suddenly filled the room. Every light on the control panel began flashing frantically.

'There's a hole in the outer shell!' the chief technician yelled in panic. 'Oil's getting in!'

'What?' Fearo screamed. That was impossible. The ship was supposed to be invulnerable. 'Surface you idiot!' he snapped. 'Unless you want us all to drown in oil, surface!'

The technician didn't need to be told twice. He pointed the *Seth*'s nose upwards and started the motors whining at top speed to get above ground as quickly as possible.

James and Cleo were on the catwalk when the nose of the *Seth* shot upwards. They grabbed at the pipes to keep from falling as the deck slanted and became too steep for them to stand on. This was what James had been hoping for – Fearo would have to get out of the pipeline to repair his crippled ship.

He gestured to a hatchway above their heads. 'That must lead out of the ship,' he explained to Cleo. 'As soon as we come to the surface, we make a break for it.'

Cleo nodded. Then she pointed to the rising oil in the engine room. It was getting unbearably hot in there. She and James were dripping with sweat. Let's just hope that we get to the surface before that gets to boiling point!'

CHAPTER 16

Meanwhile in the Crypt . . .

Trevor screamed as he slid down the rocky slope in pitch darkness. He screamed even louder when he hit bottom. Rubbing himself, he staggered weakly to his feet. He could make out nothing in the darkness except for the pain he felt in his behind.

'It's all Bond's fault,' he decided. 'Here I was, going for help for him, heedless of the consequences for myself, and what happens? I hurt myself. He's probably laughing at me, as usual. This is the last time I try to save his life. Definitely the last time.' Feeling very sorry for himself, he looked around. It didn't help him at all, since he couldn't see anything. 'I'm not enjoying this,' he said. 'Not one bit.'

'But I am,' said a voice that sounded like the wind blowing through leaves. Or like the voice of someone who hadn't spoken in a long time. About three thousand years.

Trevor felt his knees knocking together. 'Who . . . who's there?' he asked in a quiet, shaky voice.

'Me.' There was the sudden scratch of a

match being struck, and then a flare of bright-
ness that hurt Trevor's eyes. When he could
see again, he wished he couldn't.

Standing in front of him, holding a burning
torch, was a hideous figure. It was wrapped
entirely in bandages and smelled terrible!

'Mummy!' Trevor screeched.

'Right on the first guess,' the horrible figure
agreed. 'Amenhotep, to be exact.'

Trevor wondered if he was going to faint.
Then his legs decided for him. He rushed off
into the darkness, running away from the light
as fast as he could. With a throaty laugh, the
mummy charged after him.

'Let's be logical about this,' IQ said, trying to
sound firm, as they walked back along the
corridor.

'You be logical,' Phoebe replied. 'I'm going to
scream.' She started to take a deep breath, but
Tracy clamped her hands over Phoebe's mouth.

'Don't waste the air,' she said. 'We have to
save what's left in case James brings help.'

'That won't help,' Gordo put in as they
re-entered the treasure room. 'The air's most
unrighteous in here. It's going faster than a
ripping wave.'

'I fear that your friend is correct,' Professor
Gheeza agreed. He'd loosened his collar and
removed his tie and jacket, but he was still
perspiring freely. 'It is so hot in here. And so
hard to breathe.'

'Listen to me,' IQ said. Because of the lack of oxygen, he had to take several deep breaths. 'The mummy must have come from somewhere. And it must have gone somewhere.'

'Right,' Phoebe agreed. 'Like the afterlife or something. And I don't want to go after it!'

'No,' Tracy said, seeing what IQ was getting at. 'As soon as it thought we were going to jump it, it ran away. I think IQ's right. It's not really a mummy at all.'

'Then where did it vanish to?' Phoebe objected. 'It's certainly not in this tomb right now.'

'Think!' IQ said. 'Those tomb robbers got into the entrance passageway without breaking the seal on the outer door or the one on the treasure room. So did that mummy. There has to be a secret tunnel into the passageway from somewhere else.'

Tracy laughed, realizing what that meant. 'And if it leads *into* the passage, it must lead *out* as well!' She looked at IQ. 'But can we find it in time?'

'Not in here,' IQ replied 'We have to go back and search the passage.'

Tracy picked up the torch. 'Let's go to it.' She looked over at Gordo. 'Can you help the Professor through?' she asked. 'The clue might be in the carvings, and he's the only one who can read them.'

Gordo stood up. After a couple of deep

breaths, he nodded. 'Lead the way,' he told her. 'We'll be right behind you.'

With a churning of the sand, the *Seth* broke through to the surface. The engines were turned off, and James saw with great relief that the oil had stopped filling the engine room. Even as he and Cleo prised open the hatch the oil level started to go down.

Just as the hatch popped open Pharaoh Fearo and three of his guards charged into the engine room. The furious Pharaoh pointed at James.

'There's the trouble,' he howled. 'I should have guessed it – Bond and that girl again!' He then saw what James was doing. 'They're escaping!' he screamed. 'After them, you jackal-brained dolts!'

The three guards tried to obey, but there was a layer of oil covering the floor. When they started to run, their feet skidded on the oil and they went down in a dirty tangle on the floor. James looked back from the open hatchway and grinned.

'I think we've given them the slip,' he told Cleo.

He closed and fastened the hatch behind them. Then he jumped down to the sand beside Cleo. Looking around, he saw several tents by an oasis. One of them had collapsed in the *Seth*'s wake but the others were still standing.

'Where there are tents, there are inhabi-tents,' James joked. 'Maybe they'll be friendly.'

He and Cleo set off at a run towards the inviting oasis. As they reached the circle of tents several large Bedouins rose from behind the tents, where they have been hiding.

James skidded to a halt. 'Can you help us?' he asked urgently.

'By all means,' the first Arab agreed. Then he drew a large curved sword and grinned at them. 'We can help you find your way to Allah.'

James eyed the sharp blade. 'I get your point,' he said. 'Can I at least explain?'

The air seemed to be getting even more stale in the dark passageway. IQ used his fingers to feel for indentations or hidden switches in the carvings.

Tracy was next to him, trying to make some sense of the paintings. They all seemed to suggest death – as an all-too-real possibility right now. Phoebe was punching anything that looked like it might be a secret button or lever. Gordo held the almost unconscious Professor Gheeza near the wall. The elderly scholar was reading the inscriptions as fast as he could. Very little of what he was saying made any sense to Gordo.

Then the Professor gave a cry. At first Gordo thought it was because he was dying. Then he realized that the old man was actually laughing.

'So, share the joke,' he said.

'The secret exit . . .,' gasped the Professor. 'It was staring us in the face all the time.' Then, out of breath, he collapsed.

'Bogus,' Gordo groaned. 'He's out cold – right when he'd figured out the answer.'

'What did he mean?' Phoebe asked, fighting for her own breath. 'There are hundreds of faces in these carvings.'

'But only one of Amenhotep!' Tracy exclaimed. 'And it's his tomb!' She staggered over to the huge carving of the dead pharaoh. The face – that was it! Her eyes were having trouble focusing, but her fingers were able to find the face. The answer had to be here somewhere . . . She felt the eyes. One pupil seemed to be just a little odd. She jabbed at it with her finger. 'Oh, rats,' she muttered. 'I broke a nail.'

Then there was a slight grinding noise and the wall pivoted on a hidden point. A blast of fresh air shot over them. They all breathed in gratefully.

Suddenly they heard the sound of something moving through the darkness ahead of them. Then, with a horrible, terrified scream, Trevor fell backwards through the opening and landed right on top of IQ.

CHAPTER 17

Battle at the Oasis

James and Cleo were led by the Arab swords-
men to Sheikh Hassan. He was sitting beside
his collapsed tent, watching several of his men
trying to raise it again. He looked around,
and when he saw James, his eyes sparkled with
anger.

'So,' he hissed. 'You are the creep who top-
pled my tent. And right before the start of my
favourite show, too!'

Before James could reply, Cleo darted forward. 'Oh, no, mighty ruler,' she said, throwing herself to her knees. 'James is a friend.'

The Sheikh stared at her in astonishment.
He was not used to seeing women without
veils, much less such a pretty one. His anger
seemed to vanish. He reluctantly looked from
her to James.

'Well, if you're telling the truth, then who is
responsible for attacking me in my home?' the
Sheikh asked.

James spoke up. 'It's the criminal who calls
himself Pharaoh Fearo,' he explained. 'He has
a special craft, a subterranean battleship he
calls the *Seth*. He's tunnelled under the Red
Sea and into your land.'

'Has he indeed?' the Sheikh asked. 'And why on earth has he done that?'

'To steal your oil,' James told him. 'Unless we stop him, he'll rob you blind. And unless I can get my hands on his machine, my friends will die.'

'Stealing my oil?' Hassan roared furiously. 'By all the stars in the heavens, this man will pay for his crimes!' Then he calmed down a little. 'But if he has a vessel that can burrow under the desert sands, how can I hope to stop him?'

'Well,' James said, 'I have an idea. But I'll need transportation. Do you have some camels I could borrow?'

'Camels?' The Sheikh burst out laughing. 'I think you've been watching too many old movies, my friend.' He put an arm around James's shoulder and led both him and Cleo through the camp. Just beyond the circle of tents was another circle – this time of vehicles.

There were two tanks, several half-track trucks, a dozen or more Jeeps, and two heavy-duty cars. There were also several motorcycles.

'Where did you get these?' Cleo asked.

Sheikh Hassan shrugged. 'Army surplus,' he told her. 'You'd be amazed what a few dollars can buy.' He gestured towards the parked vehicles. 'Take your pick!'

James grinned. 'I think I'm going to like this part!'

*

Pharaoh Fearo glared angrily at this men. 'Well?' he asked coldly. 'Are you finished yet?'

The chief technician nodded. 'We've managed to clean out all of the oil,' he said. 'And we've made a patch over the hole in the rear. But it won't last long without a complete tune-up.'

Fearo's face was dark with anger. 'May all the dogs and tigers of the underworld gnaw on young Bond's bones!' he roared. 'Very well, prepare to return to base.'

One of the guards posted to watch the desert for any further signs of Bond gave a cry. He pointed with his sword. A large cloud of dust was visible and it seemed to be growing closer. 'Someone is coming.'

'That's obvious, you clod,' the Pharaoh replied. 'And I think it's safe to say it's not likely to be a welcome wagon.' He glared at the chief technician. 'Get the *Seth* under way. Now!'

'It'll take a few minutes,' the man replied as he vanished inside.

Pharaoh Fearo slammed his fist down on his ship. 'Curse that interfering Bond,' he muttered. 'But we'll see about slowing him down.' He yelled at the four guards on duty, 'Make certain that whoever that is doesn't get in.' Then he dived below into the control room. 'Ready the sand torpedoes!' he ordered.

James grinned over his shoulder at Cleo as

he led the charge of Sheikh Hassan's troops. He was riding one of the motorcycles, which the Sheikh's men had kept in perfect condition. The engine had been sealed, making it sandproof, and its throaty roar howled in the air.

Behind them came the Sheikh and his men. The armoured cars bounced along, as did the half-tracks. The tanks were quite a lot slower, though, and probably would miss most of the battle – assuming that they even reached the break in the pipeline before Fearo managed to get away.

Then Cleo pointed. Just ahead of them, James could see a glint of gold in the desert sunlight. It could only be the *Seth*, still on the surface!

'Now we've got him,' James laughed.

'Look out!' Cleo yelled in his ear.

Something was ploughing just under the surface of the sand and heading straight towards them. It looked uncomfortably like the wake of a torpedo at sea. Then James remembered that the mad monarch had called the *Seth* a tunnelling warship.

'It's a sand torpedo!' he shouted. He jerked the bike around in a tight circle, and the missile just missed his front wheel.

The Sheikh's men also scattered their vehicles out of the line of fire. The torpedo sliced through the sand until it came to a tall date palm. The tree exploded into smithereens and fell like burning rain all around them.

But the blast had done its job. It had bought the Pharaoh the extra time he needed to escape. With a loud hum of its motors, the *Seth* vanished back underground.

'He's getting away!' Cleo cried.

'Not yet he isn't,' James promised her. Revving the motor as high as it would go, James ran the motorcycle directly towards the hole the *Seth* had vanished into. As James jumped into the pit, Cleo gave a cry. When the motorcycle's wheels slammed down on the smooth metal of the pipeline, the last few drops of oil from the spill James had caused sent the bike into a skid. James fought to regain control, then roared down the tunnel after the mechanical mole.

CHAPTER 18

Unwrapping the Mummy

IQ pushed Trevor off and managed to get to his feet again. With the blast of fresh air from the secret tunnel, they could all breathe again. Gasping in lungfuls of air, Gordo, Phoebe, and Tracy were soon looking much better. Even Professor Gheeza seemed to be recovering. Only Trevor was still pale and shaking.

'I'm sorry about using that shovel of yours,' he told IQ. 'I didn't know it would cause a cave-in! Honest!'

'So that's what happened.' IQ wiped off his glasses and replaced them. For the first time in hours he could see properly – or as well as could be expected, considering that one lens was still cracked. 'I ought to use that shovel on your head.'

'But I'm being chased by a mummy!' Trevor howled. 'It's Amenhotep, and he wants to turn me into a mummy, too. I'm too young to be a mummy!'

Gordo grinned. 'The fake mummy dude, eh?' Now that they had seen how the creature pulled its vanishing tricks, a lot of their terror had disappeared. 'I'd say a showdown is way overdue.' He led the charge back into the secret passageway.

The mummy had been enjoying itself chasing the panic-stricken Trevor around the tunnels. But things had changed. Four very determined-looking people blocked its path. It came to a halt and tried to run away, but it was too late. Gordo hit it in the knees and Tracy caught it in the chest. It went down with a yelp, and IQ and Phoebe sat on it.

'Let's check out the face behind the mask,' Tracy said, grabbing one of the loose ends of the decaying bandage. With a jerk of her wrist, she ripped it free.

'Ow!' the mummy cried.

They all gasped in astonishment. Professor Gheeza staggered up, determined not to be left out of this. 'Farid!' he exclaimed. 'What are you doing dressed up like that?'

IQ pointed at the foreman accusingly. 'I suspect he's an agent of Pharaoh Fearo,' he said. 'And I bet he's the one responsible for all of the sabotage.'

The old Professor glared angrily at his assistant. 'In that case, you're fired,' he said.

Gordo used some of the bandages to tie up Farid. 'We should leave you in the crypt,' he said. 'Maybe they'd dig you up in another three thousand years.'

At the thought, Farid fainted.

'This passageway leads downwards,' Tracy

said, taking the lead. 'Let's see where it ends up. It might lead to a way out – or to James.'

After about fifteen minutes of wandering through the tunnels, they came to the great throne room.

'Awesome,' Gordo said. 'I bet Indiana Jones would love this place!'

The large room was deserted and they spread out to take a good look around. A few minutes later Phoebe called to the others and they all rushed over to find the secret door that Fearo had left open.

'This is getting more and more interesting,' IQ commented. 'Let's see where this leads.'

They came out in the giant cavern and stared around in astonishment. 'Some pad,' Tracy said. 'I wonder how much rent he pays for this place?'

There was the sound of rushing air and then the throb of running motors. It came from farther down the cavern and they ran off to investigate. They barely paused at the giant statues of the Pharaoh, but when they saw the huge gold machine they froze in their tracks.

'Amazing!' IQ breathed. 'A subterranean burrower.'

The hatchway opened up and Pharaoh Fearo clambered out. He did a double-take when he saw the four youngsters rushing towards his ship. 'More of that accursed Bond's friends?' he cried in disbelief. Then he jumped from the ship and ran for the side wall of the platform.

Gordo was the first to reach the *Seth*. He leapt on to the deck just as the first of the technicians was trying to climb up the ladder. Smoke billowed out from inside. It was obvious that the ship was crippled.

'Your turn to suffer,' Gordo told the startled man. Then he slammed the hatch down on his head. There was the sound of a body falling down as Gordo threw the locks into place. 'How about this?' he called to the others. 'Canned rats!'

Tracy and IQ had gone after Fearo, but he reached another of his secret panels before they could catch up to him. Behind it was an elevator that Fearo jumped into. 'Going up!' he called. The doors slammed shut in Tracy's face, and with a whine of motors the Pharaoh made his escape.

'You can never catch a lift when you need one,' Tracy sighed.

'Listen!' Phoebe called out, pointing down the tunnel. They could all hear the loud roar of a powerful engine. Then James and Cleo shot out of the tunnel on the bike. James brought the machine to a halt, its motor still idling.

'Fearo's escaping,' IQ said quickly. 'He's taken the lift to the surface.'

'There must be another way up there,' James said. 'He'd never leave just one exit.'

'There are a number of side tunnels,' IQ said. 'Some must lead to the surface.'

'Right,' James agreed. Gunning the motor, he sent the bike roaring through the cavern to the throne room. Cleo hung on as James sped through the secret door and across the empty throne room. Beyond the throne room the ground sloped up, and they started to pass by a series of passageways crossing the one they were in.

'Check for signs that one of these leads to the surface!' James told Cleo. 'We have to stop Fearo from getting away.'

He slowed the bike as they came to each passageway. At the third one, Cleo grinned. 'According to one inscription, this will come out somewhere near the Nile,' she told him.

James smiled back. 'Going up.'

A group of tourists were making their way around the ancient ruins of the temple of Rameses II. This massive temple was as impressive as it was huge, and many cameras clicked away as a guide explained all of the sights.

One young mother was trying to keep her six-year-old son in line. Suddenly, he pointed. 'Look at the funny man!' he said. 'He's wearing funny clothing!'

'Behave yourself, Stanley,' his mother said. 'And don't be rude! I'm sure you wouldn't like it if that man made fun of your clothes.'

'That man' was actually Pharaoh Fearo. He had slipped out of his lift and was rushing down towards the Nile and a speedboat he had moored there. Like most crooks, he was always prepared for trouble.

'And over there,' the guide said, pointing, 'is a fine example of an ancient Egyptian motorcycle.' Then he did a double take as he realized what he had said.

James and Cleo rode the bike quickly through the crowd of tourists. Several of the visitors snapped off pictures. Their friends back home would never believe this!

Cleo pointed ahead of them. 'There he is!'

James saw the fleeing Pharaoh and sped towards him. Hearing the sound of the motorcycle, Fearo glanced back. With a muttered curse, he jumped out of James's way. Then he clambered up onto the base of one of the great stone sphinxes. As the cycle went past James and Cleo leapt from it on to the sphinx. James's fingers barely managed to grip the edge of the statue. Then he hung there, fighting for a foothold. Cleo had managed to hang onto his shoulders, but they couldn't hold on for long.

Fearo gave an evil grin and drew the sword he carried. 'You've interfered with my plans just once too often,' he said. 'And now I'll make certain you never do again.'

James's foot finally found a crack in the broken stone. Now he could risk letting go with one hand. He grabbed the red water flask he still had hooked on his belt. Gripping its strap, James waited until Fearo charged at them.

111

Then he swung the metal flask around with all of his strength.

It caught the startled Pharaoh on the chin. With a glazed expression, he dropped his sword and collapsed into a heap on the stones.

James pulled himself up onto the base of the sphinx. He and Cleo looked down at the unconscious criminal with satisfaction.

'Well, I always knew his plans were bad,' James told Cleo. 'In fact, they sphinx.'

CHAPTER 19

All Wrapped Up

That evening, James and his friends were finally able to relax. Professor Gheeza was looking forward to exploring all of the underground passageways that Pharaoh Fearo had made. IQ was impatient to take a good look at the *Seth*. Even Mr Milbanks seemed to be relatively happy about how the whole affair had turned out.

'The only person who was completely unhappy was Trevor. When he had recovered from his horrible ordeal, he saw that James was a hero once again. 'It's not fair,' he muttered to himself. 'I tried to save them all and I end up looking like an idiot. Meanwhile Bond is the golden boy again. It isn't fair. It just isn't fair.'

Cleo and James had celebrated their friendship by going out to dinner. James was more than happy with the way things had gone, and he was sorry to have to leave Egypt so soon. Now he stood in his room looking down at the Nile by moonlight, his friends with him. The next day they'd be returning to Warfield.

'It's going to seem tame back at school after this,' he told them. 'I never knew that archaeology could be this much fun.'

'Personally,' Tracy answered, 'I thought things like this only happened to Indiana Jones!'

'You know what they always say,' IQ told her. 'Truth is stranger than fiction.'

Gordo grinned. 'Well, I just hope they keep that loony Pharaoh locked away for a good long time. Several dynasties, maybe.'

'Yeah,' Phoebe agreed. 'Could you believe that he told the police that they couldn't arrest him because he was the rightful ruler of all Egypt?'

James gave his friends a smile. 'Well, he was always a great believer in old proverbs. I think the one that applies in his case is, all's Pharaoh in love and war.'

YOUNG INDIANA JONES AND THE
GHOSTLY RIDER
by William McCay

**Did King Arthur really exist? Who were the Knights of the
Round Table? Where was the legendary Castle of Camelot?**

Such questions are not of the slightest interest to Young
ndiana Jones . . . that is until he meets Cerdic Sandyford at
the Charenton Academy. Cerdic's father owns a South
Vales colliery, but goes to great lengths to ensure his miners
are properly looked after.

When Indy and Cerdic arrive at the pit they discover a
ruthless rival who will stop at nothing to sabotage his
'caring approach'. Dynamite, cave-ins and ghostly
encounters are all taken in his stride in one of Indy's most
mysterious and dangerous adventures yet.

YOUNG INDIANA JONES AND THE RUBY CROSS
by William McCay

**After his many adventures overseas, you would expect Young
Indy to take a break somewhere quiet, restful and danger-
free!**

Young Indiana Jones is relacing in New York City. But
very quickly a chance meeting with a long-lost friend and
he discovery of a mysterious medieval relic lead to just one
thing . . . trouble!

,000 years before this story begins, a Norman knight places
a curse on a sacred cross. Thus, whoever steals it and
whoever loses it must die. With the cross now missing,
Young Indy begins a race against time to retrieve the relic
and to save his friend who owns it.

YOUNG INDIANA JONES AND THE PRINCESS
OF PERIL
by Les Martin

Aboard the Paris–St Petersburg Express as it races through the night, Young Indiana Jones helps a boy to evade the secret police.

So begins another adventure for Indy – but his new-found friend soon realizes the authorities are not so easily thrown off the track. Pre-revolution Russia is a very dangerous place, especially for those who dare to speak out against the Czar . . .

When Indy steps in, the might of the Russian Empire is thrown against him, and even he begins to wonder if there is any way out of this one.

YOUNG INDIANA JONES AND THE
CRUSADER'S CROWN
by Les Martin

On the trail of a medieval manuscript in the South of France, Young Indiana Jones finds himself drawn into the dangerous streets of the Marseille underworld.

But Indy has somebody to 'help' him – his least favourite travelling companion in the entire world, Thornton N. Thornton. Together they unravel the mystery of the manuscript, to discover they are not the only people with an interest in its message.

They soon become involved in a sinister conspiracy that could lead to a new reign of terror throughout the whole of France . . .

BATMAN: THE BLACK EGG OF ATLANTIS

Neal Barrett

The discovery of an ancient artifact from Atlantis sparks a major outbreak of crime and violence in Gotham City. Shrouded by darkness for centuries, the black egg of Atlantis seems to exert a sinister hold over Gotham's population.

So alluring is its evil that the avian master of crime, Penguin, comes out of hiding to steal it, vowing to bring death to the Dark Knight in the process. The hours tick towards a midnight showdown when Batman will face a battle to the death – bat against bird.

BATMAN: I, WEREWOLF

Ed Gorman

Gotham City is trapped in the jaws of terror as its streets become the hunting-ground of a mysterious werewolf. Out of the night Robin and his mentor Batman come to track this beast, vowing to save the city from its vicious attacks.

As Robin is drawn deeper into the case, he discovers a dark secret about the werewolf that he must keep from Batman. But without Batman's help, can Robin stop the rampage of the killer wolf before it strikes again?

ROBIN HOOD PRINCE OF THIEVES
Simon Green

The legend lives on. Like a flaming arrow, Robin of Locksley emerges from the shadows of Sherwood Forest to blaze a path for the poor and downtrodden. With a mighty band of fighting men by his side – Friar Tuck, Will Scarlet, the noble Saracen called Azeem, and others – Robin wages a magnificent war against the vicious Sheriff of Nottingham . . . and an equally passionate campaign for the heart of the beautiful Maid Marian. Wielding his bow and arrow with deadly accuracy, Robin of Locksley transforms himself into a new kind of hero.

THE ADDAMS FAMILY
by Elizabeth Faucher

You haven't lived unless you've met the Adams Family! There's Morticia, the loving, caring mother, Gomez, the devoted but manic father, and their children Pugsley and Wednesday. Pugsley collects road signs, and Wednesday's favourite toy is a headlsss doll. Then, of course, there's Thing, the Addams Family's pet hand, who is always willing to lend one, when two just aren't enough. With the return of Uncle Fester, the long-lost brother of Gomez, after twenty-five years' absence, the family is complete once again. However, he may look like Uncle Fester, he may even sound like him, but can he really be the missing uncle?

LUKE MANIA! JASON FEVER
Jeff Rovin

Get to know the *real* Brandon and Dylan! The superstars of Beverly Hills, 90210 get personal – and reveal who they really are off-camera . . .

LUKE PERRY

You love him as bad boy Dylan McKay. But would you believe the real Luke Perry is sweet and *shy*? What secrets does he hide behind those sexy eyes? Get the facts on this cool hunk.

JASON PRIESTLEY

He plays the almost too-gorgeous-to-be-true Brandon Walsh. But off-camera he's more than irresistible – he's positively *hot*! Discover the wild side of this super-sensitive sensation.